"I have no idea how to work this thing."

Justin grinned. "Help is on the way."

He crossed the room with the wineglasses, gave Bailey hers and tapped their glasses together. He leaned down and kissed her lips. "Hmm, sweet."

Bailey's insides vibrated. She couldn't imagine what making love to him would feel like. Inadvertently, she moaned.

Justin tipped his head toward her in question.

"The wine…it's really good." At least she was still thinking on her feet.

"Glad you like it."

He turned his attention to the system, pressed a few buttons, and Luther Vandross's sultry crooning wafted around them.

Justin took Bailey's glass from her hand and placed it on the side table. "Dance with me."

Bailey sputtered a nervous laugh. "Dance with you?"

"Yes." He stepped to her, slid one arm around her waist and eased her close. "Like this," he murmured against her hair.

Her eyes drifted closed when she rested her head against his chest and she silently prayed that he didn't feel her body trembling. Her pulse roared in her ears.

Dear Reader,

Welcome to the latest installment of the Lawsons of Louisiana series. You've met several of the members of this dynamic clan, shared in the intrigue, their complicated loves and exciting lives. Now I want to introduce you to the youngest member, the sensual Justin Lawson. Much like his siblings Lee Ann, Dominique, Desiree and Rafe, Justin intends to forge his own path, his way. And like his siblings, when he sees something he wants, he goes after it. What he wants is the heart and soul of Bailey Sinclair. However, it won't be easy to convince the very independent Bailey that it's time for someone to love her, to care for her the way that she has taken care of her siblings.

I love writing about the Lawsons, who split their time between Baton Rouge and Sag Harbor. The locales are perfect backdrops, and the complications that their status and money afford them are great fodder for sexy, thrilling and satisfying stories that I hope each of you enjoy.

So sit back, relax, grab a glass of wine and enjoy the journey to love with Justin Lawson and Bailey Sinclair. I guarantee that you will be glad you did.

Also, be sure to check out all of the books in the Lawsons of Louisiana series. There are plenty more to come.

Until next time,

Donna

THE WAY *You* LOVE ME

DONNA HILL

HARLEQUIN® KIMANI™ ROMANCE

Recycling programs
for this product may
not exist in your area.

ISBN-13: 978-0-373-86389-1

The Way You Love Me

Copyright © 2015 by Donna Hill

For questions and comments about the quality of this book please contact us
at CustomerService@Harlequin.com.

Printed in U.S.A.

Donna Hill began writing novels in 1990. Since that time she has had more than forty titles published, which include full-length novels and novellas. Two of her novels and one novella were adapted for television. She has won numerous awards for her body of work. She is also the editor of five novels, two of which were nominated for awards. She easily moves from romance to erotica, horror, comedy and women's fiction. She was the first recipient of the *RT Book Reviews* Trailblazer Award and won the *RT Book Reviews* Career Achievement Award, and she currently teaches writing at the Frederick Douglass Creative Arts Center.

Donna lives in Brooklyn with her family. Visit her website at donnahill.com.

Books by Donna Hill
Harlequin Kimani Romance

Love Becomes Her
If I Were Your Woman
After Dark
Sex and Lies
Seduction and Lies
Temptation and Lies
Longing and Lies
Private Lessons
Spend My Life with You
Secret Attraction
Sultry Nights
Everything Is You
Mistletoe, Baby
The Way You Love Me

Visit the Author Profile page
at Harlequin.com for more titles

Chapter 1

The stack of overdue notices glared accusingly up at Bailey from the backdrop of her wobbly kitchen table. Credit cards. Car payment. Student loans. Overdraft fees. They all read the same: "Dear Ms. Sinclair: Overdue. Demand for payment. Respond in ten days." One after the other. What was not in the pile was what she needed most—the scholarship letter that would pave the way for her to return to law school in the fall.

She'd applied for every scholarship that she could conceivably be eligible for but had yet to receive a positive response. For years she'd put her life on hold for her family. This was her time, but now with the fall semester beginning in just over four months, her goal of completing her law degree was becoming more of a dream than a reality.

Bailey stuck the notices back in their envelopes and stared out of her third-floor apartment window at the approaching dusk that had turned the horizon into a soft rosey hue. She drew in a long breath. Sitting there wishing things were different wasn't going to get the bills paid. She had a job to get to, and her shift at the Mercury Lounge would not wait for her. She pushed back from the table, and it rocked in response.

The Mercury Lounge was the hub for the who's who of Baton Rouge, Louisiana. On any given night the patrons ranged from the average customer to politicians, business entrepreneurs, and entertainment and sports figures. She enjoyed her job. Meeting new people, listening to their stories and their problems fed her legal mind, and, of course, there were the regulars who came in to simply get free advice. Too bad that enjoying what she did for a living wasn't enough to keep her afloat.

Fortunately, she had her side hustle with her best friend, Addison Matthews, whose business was catering parties for the rich and fabulous. The extra income certainly helped, but it was no longer enough.

Addison swore that if Bailey would loosen up and give a play to one of those sexy, wealthy men that were always hitting on her, she could put an end to the demand notices and collection calls and return to school. Not to mention the perks of having a man to warm that big empty bed of hers at night. Bailey had stopped listening to Addison. She knew all too well what running after money could do. It destroyed lives, and the trait ran in her family like a string of corrupted DNA, and she vowed to break the chain. That meant doing it on her own no matter how difficult that might be.

Bailey grabbed her purse, a light jacket and her keys then headed out, hoping on her way downstairs that her ten-year-old Honda—that was five years old when she bought it—would start, just as the ringing of her cell phone slowed her steps. She glanced at the name on the face of the phone. *Her sister Tory.* Her stomach knotted.

"Hey, sis." She threw up a silent prayer. "What's up?"

"Hi, Bailey. I know you're probably getting ready for work."

"I'm on my way out the door."

"Um, you know I hate to ask…"

"What is it, Tory? What do you need?"

"You don't have to say it like that," she whined petulantly.

Bailey silently counted to ten. "What do you need, sis?"

"I'm behind on my rent."

"Again? Tory…"

"I just had more expenses than I thought this month."

"More shopping and partying."

"That's not fair!"

"How much, Tory?"

"Twelve-hundred dollars."

Bailey's jaw tightened. She did a quick calculation in her head. Giving her sister twelve hundred dollars would dig deep into her savings, set her back on her own plans. But Tory was her younger sister, and she swore when their mother died that she would take care of her sisters, no matter what. "Fine. I'll put a check in the mail."

"Thank you, Bailey. I really appreciate it. I swear I'm going to do better, sis."

"Sure. Listen, I gotta go."

"Okay. Thanks again. Love you."

"Bye, Tory." She disconnected the call, and her shoulders slumped.

Bailey arrived at the Mercury Lounge, and the instant that she stepped through the doors she felt the energy and knew that it would be a busy night. Busy was good. Busy meant plenty of customers and lots of tips. She finger-waved and lifted her chin in salute to several of her co-workers as she strolled through the lowest level of the tri-level venue. She still had about an hour before her shift started and plenty to do until then.

Although she was originally hired as a mixologist three years earlier, the owner, Vincent Mercury, "saw something" in Bailey, and when an opportunity presented itself, he offered her the assistant manager spot with a nice bump in her salary. Combined with her duties of running the bars, things started looking up for her financially. That all changed, with one thing after the other.

"Vince in back?" Bailey asked Kim, the Friday night hostess.

"He went upstairs to check on the setup in the private dining room. We have that party tonight."

Bailey squeezed her eyes shut for an instant. She'd totally forgotten. "Right." She should have come in earlier. "Guess I'd better get busy." She continued on toward the back offices tucked along a narrow corridor. She dug her keys out of her purse and unlocked her makeshift office that had been transformed from a storage room that was about a half inch bigger than a walk-in closet. The tight space was big enough for a desk the size of a small kitchen table, two chairs and a six-drawer file cabinet. She'd had the room painted white and hung a floor-to-ceiling mirror on one wall to give the illusion of space. A couple of potted plants, two wall paintings and a framed photo of her and her siblings made the space cozy without feeling overcrowded.

Bailey unlocked her desk drawer, put her purse in and locked it again. She opened the cover of her laptop and powered it up. The first thing that she needed to check was that all the staff that was scheduled for the night shift was accounted for and had not called out. Then she had to plan the scheduling for the week, verify the details for an upcoming local company luncheon and approve an order for linens that was requested by the floor manager. By the time she was done, it was about fifteen minutes before her shift at the bar was to begin, but she wanted to make a quick stop up to the private dining room and make sure that Vince didn't need her for anything before she got behind the bar.

The private dining room was on the third level. One wall was glass and looked out over the city's horizon. The space seated fifty comfortably, and for bigger events one wall retracted to join the next room that could accommodate another one hundred guests.

When Bailey got off the escalator the waitstaff was

fully engaged in preparation. She spotted Vince on the far side of the room, giving directions while checking his clipboard.

"Hey, looks like you have everything under control," she said, sidling up to him.

He barely glanced up at her over the rim of his glasses. "There's always something that doesn't get done," he said, and his tone clearly relayed his annoyance.

"What happened?"

"The centerpieces were supposed to be crystal goblets with white orchids floating in water." His brow cinched as he ran his hand through his golden-blond hair.

Bailey looked at the centerpieces, which were lovely but clearly not what Vincent requested. Instead, they were long-stemmed calla lilies in slender vases. And she realized immediately what the issue was. Even though the centerpieces were beautiful to look at, the size and type of flower obstructed the diners' views of each other at the table. Bailey folded her arms and tried to think of an option.

"I have an idea." She didn't wait for Vincent to respond. She began giving instructions to the staff to take the centerpieces off the tables, load them onto a cart and two of them were to come with her to the basement storage room. She pulled out her cell phone and called Addison.

"Hey, Addie, listen, we're in a bind. Remember those goblets that you used for your last catering job?"

"Yep. What's up?"

"I need to use them for tonight. We still have them in our storage room here at the Mercury Lounge."

"Sure. Not a problem. You didn't need to call me for that."

"I wanted to make sure it was okay."

"Listen, I appreciate you being able to hold on to my stuff for me. With the catering jobs getting bigger and bigger, I'm running out of space in my apartment. Even though it's been more cost-effective to purchase what I need instead of renting, it's taking a toll on my square footage." She laughed.

"I hear that. Anyway, thanks, girl. Gotta run."

"Talk to you later."

Once they reached the storage room in the basement, Bailey instructed the staff to box up the vases after removing the calla lilies. She laid the plants out on a long table, found a pair of scissors and started cutting the lilies down to size. Shortly after, the lilies were floating in the goblets and were being placed back on the tables.

"I don't know what I'd do without you," Vincent said, his gray eyes crinkling at the corners with his smile. He gave her quick kiss on the cheek.

Bailey blinked in surprise. "Drive yourself crazy." She patted his shoulder. "I have to get downstairs. My shift has already started."

"Thanks again," he called out.

She waved away his thanks and hurried off, pushing the impromptu cheek kiss to the back of her mind.

By the time Bailey returned to the ground level, the line for the early diners to be seated had grown. Every stool at the bar was taken, and the two bartenders were working their magic.

Bailey came around to the entrance of the bar. "Hey, Mellie, hectic already, I see," she said and took her black apron from the hook and tied it around her waist.

"Girl, you would think this was the last stop in town," she joked. She poured a splash of top-shelf rum over ice, dropped in a slice of lime and spun away toward her customer.

Bailey took a quick inventory of supplies and made sure that the snack bowls on the counter were freshened and full. Then she went to work, mixing and joking with the customers. She loved the teasing games she played with them, especially her regulars. It was all harmless fun, and it made the evenings fly by. And, of course, there were the more serious-minded conversations on politics, religion, cheating spouses and significant others and the customary legal questions. It all came with the territory.

She'd been going nonstop for about an hour when two seats in her section opened. One was quickly occupied. She took a cloth from beneath the bar counter and walked over to her new customer. She did what she always did: wiped down the counter, placed a bowl of snacks on the bar, shot him with her best smile and took his order.

"Welcome to the Mercury Lounge. What can I get for you?"

Carl Hurley scooped up a handful of nuts and tossed them in his mouth. He chewed slowly. "I'm actually waiting on my buddy until our table is ready. But how 'bout a Corona while I wait?"

"Not a problem."

She turned away and went to get the beer and a glass. When she returned, the empty seat was occupied, and the two men were in an animated conversation. She was all ready to get into her routine when he turned and looked at her. Something hit her, like a flash or a shock or something; she couldn't be sure. And for a moment she didn't breathe when the light caught in his eyes, and he smiled. Not a full smile but halfway, just the corner of his mouth. She blinked and placed the bottle of beer and glass in front of her customer and forced herself to concentrate.

"Good evening. And what can I get you?"

The dark of his eyes moved really slowly over her face, and every inch that was exposed to his perusal heated. The pulse in her throat tripled its beat.

"Hmm, bourbon. Neat. Four Roses."

"Coming right up." She spun away, and her knees were gelatin-shaky. She drew in a breath and scanned the shelf for the bottles of bourbon, missing them twice before she recognized them for what they were. At least the glasses were right in front of her. She brought the glass and the bottle of Four Roses bourbon and placed the glass in front of him. "Say when."

The warm brown liquid slid from the mouth of the bottle into the wide opening of the glass with a bare splash. The heady aroma aroused the senses.

"When…"

Bailey took her eyes away from what she was doing, and her gaze bumped right against his. She lightly ran her tongue across her bottom lip as she watched him bring the glass to his nose. Inhaled. Nodded. Took a sip. "Perfect."

"Let me know if you gentlemen need anything else." She managed to tug herself away from his magnetic pull.

"You okay?" Mellie asked as she dumped glasses in the sudsy water.

"Yeah, why?"

"You seem distracted. Not your usual bouncy self."

"I'm good. A few things on my mind, that's all."

Mellie studied Bailey for a moment then shrugged. "Cool. I'm going to take my break as soon as things slow down."

"Sure."

"Wow, that guy down on the end is hot," she said under her breath.

"Who?"

"Your customer. The one with the open-collar white shirt, no tie. Don't tell me you didn't notice."

Bailey's heart thumped. "I try not to."

"Girl, you must be angling for sainthood. Give me a minute with him." She slid her eyes in his direction.

Bailey sputtered a laugh. "You need to stop."

"And why would I do that?" she teased, emphasizing every word.

Bailey shook her head in amusement and went back to work.

* * *

Justin Lawson took a sip of his drink. His gaze kept drifting back to the woman who'd served him, subtly following her every move. "How long did they say we'd have to wait for a table?"

"At least a half hour. Didn't think we needed a reservation."

Justin glanced around. The lounge was pretty full with more patrons waiting to be seated. This was the first time he'd been to the Mercury Lounge. He'd heard good things about it, but he wanted to check it out before he brought Jasmine here.

"How is that case coming that you were working on?"

Carl sucked up a laugh. "It's a mess." He tossed back the rest of his beer straight from the bottle. "The usual corporate back room dirty deals, everyone trying to out-maneuver the other." He shook his head.

Justin, like Carl, was an attorney. Both of them worked for one of the biggest law firms in Louisiana, and they both were working hard on the side to launch Justin's non-profit—The Justice Project—something that his father, Senator Branford Lawson, wasn't pleased about.

What is it about my sons, Branford had boomed at the last family gathering. *I build a legacy for them, pave the way for them and they go off and do what the hell they want anyway.* If their father had his way, both he and his older brother, Rafe, would be embroiled in the political quagmire of Washington, DC. Rafe preferred the life of a jazz musician and womanizer. Justin always believed it was just Rafe's way to piss their father off. But at least Justin, to appease his father, had agreed to take the position at the law firm Lake, Martin and Dubois, which is where he'd met Jasmine Dubois.

"Are you finished with the depositions?" Justin asked. He was almost done with his drink. He peered down the length of the bar to get Bailey's attention.

"Should be completed by the end of the next week. I tell you, man, it's been a nightmare."

"Once we get The Justice Project off the ground, we can finally start doing the kind of work that we want to do—that needs to be done."

"Not soon enough for me," Carl said.

"Refills, gentlemen?" Bailey looked from one to the other, refusing to settle on Justin's face.

"Another Corona for me."

"And you?"

Justin studied the lines of her face, the way the tips of her eyes lifted ever so slightly, the soft rise of her breasts beneath the stiff black shirt, and the warm caramel of her skin. "I'll take another." He lifted his glass. The path of his gaze led to hers.

That spark popped between them again. Bailey sucked in a breath when Justin ran his finger around the rim of his glass.

"Coming right up." She strode down the bar to retrieve the Corona from the icebox and filled a clean glass with bourbon.

"If you two get any hotter, you'll set the joint on fire," Carl teased.

Justin rolled his head toward Carl. "What are you talking about?"

"You know damn well what I'm talking about. You haven't stopped checking her out since you sat down."

"A man can look, can't he?" He reached for a handful of cocktail peanuts.

"Yeah, but Jasmine's doing her best to claim you."

Justin heaved a sigh. "Yeah, Jasmine," he murmured.

"Trouble in paradise?"

"Let's just say she would like us to be in a relationship, but I don't think it's a good idea." He slowly shook his head.

"Hmm, makes it kind of tough with her being the boss's daughter."

"Yeah…exactly."

"Here you go, gentlemen." She placed the beer and glass in front of Carl and the bourbon in front of Justin. "Is there anything else I can get you?"

"A table," Carl groused.

Bailey smiled, and Justin's insides shifted. He lifted his glass and let his gaze drop into the depth of his drink instead of the dark pools that were her eyes.

"We're always busy on Friday nights. I take it this is your first time here." She wiped down the space in front of them and refilled the snack bowl.

"It is," Justin said.

"I wouldn't want this to be your last time." She was talking to them both, but her eyes were fixed on Justin. "Let me see what I can do about getting you a table."

"We'd appreciate that…" Justin waited for her to fill the blank.

"Bailey."

"Justin."

"I'll see what I can do, Justin."

"Oh, and I'm Carl," he said, feigning offense at being ignored.

Bailey laughed lightly. "Carl."

Bailey and Justin shared a look of amusement before she walked off.

Carl's cell phone chirped. He pulled it out of his pocket, checked the face of the phone and frowned. "Matthew…" He listened, and his expression grew tighter. "Okay. Give me a half hour. Thanks." He disconnected the call and turned to Justin.

"What's up?"

"I have to go back to the office. Matthew got a call from Judge Graham's clerk. He wants us in chambers at nine tomorrow morning. You know how anal he is. I need to pull everything we have together on the obstruction case."

"Need some help?"

"Naw." Carl stood, finished off his beer and clapped Justin on the shoulder. "You stay. That's why we have first-year associates for times like this. I'll supervise, and they'll work." He lifted his chin. "Anyway, I'm sure you'll have much more fun here than back at the office." He set his beer bottle down. "Tab is on you. Later."

Justin chuckled and lifted his drink to his lips just as Bailey returned.

"I got you a table. Where's Carl?"

Justin's brow flicked. "He had to leave. Problem at the office."

"Oh, well, if you still want the table…"

He halfway shrugged. "Can I uh, order some food and sit at the bar?"

Her heart bumped in her chest. She felt slightly giddy. "Sure. I'll get you a menu. Be right back."

Justin watched her walk away and was immensely grateful for the anal Judge Graham.

Chapter 2

Justin looked over the menu. He was pleased at the extensive selections and finally settled on a porterhouse steak, grilled asparagus and risotto.

"I'll put this in right away," Bailey said. "It might be a while. Would you like an appetizer in the meantime?"

"I'm a patient man." He slowly turned his glass. "I can wait."

Bailey tried to swallow, but her throat was so dry that she choked.

Justin leaned forward and reached for her. "You okay?"

She blinked away the water that filled her eyes. Coughed. Coughed again and wished that the floor would open. She cleared her throat. Her vision cleared, and she realized that the fire on her hand was Justin's.

Bailey took a step back, slid her hand away. "I'm sorry. I'm fine. Guess something caught in my throat."

Justin sat back down. "Well, I would have been happy to resuscitate you had the need arisen."

Bailey's stomach danced. There was that half grin again as if he knew something that no one else did.

"I'll keep that in mind."

She walked down the aisle to the other end of the bar to check on the customers and refills and could barely concentrate. What in the world was her problem? She was all twisted over some guy who could be a gorgeous serial killer for all she knew.

"Bailey, can you check the couple on the end while I fix these martinis?" Mellie asked.

"Sure." That's what she needed to be doing—paying attention to her customers, making sure that the bar was running at optimum efficiency, not getting all hot and bothered over some guy.

"What's the deal with the two you were serving?"

"Oh, one of them had to leave. Business or something," she added noncommittally while she prepared the drinks.

"The one who stayed is yummy. And you know he has his eye on you. You gonna talk to him or what?"

"Mellie…I talk to all of my customers."

"You know what I mean. He's hot. I know you have some 'policy' about interacting with the customers, but come on, girl…"

Hot. That he was. Her hand still tingled from his touch. But she'd never taken bar talk beyond the bar. To her it was the doorway to trouble, and she didn't intend to open it. She talked, she joked, she provided drinks and that was all.

"There's a first time for everything," Mellie said as if reading her mind.

Bailey shook her head, returned the bottles to their place on the shelf and walked off to serve the customers.

Justin nursed his drink while keeping Bailey on his radar. Although he'd looked forward to an evening with his friend, he was actually glad that Carl got called back to work. It would give him some space to maybe get to know Bailey a little better. He sipped his drink. *Jasmine.*

When they'd met more than a year ago and went out a few times, he thought that she might be the one. Both of their fathers encouraged the relationship. Their friends thought that they were the perfect couple, but his brother, Rafe, of all people, was the only one who threw shade on the relationship. Rafe told him in no uncertain terms that Jasmine was the one "for the moment," but not forever, and that he'd know forever when it hit him. He'd laughed off his big brother's warning. Rafe was a notorious ladies' man, and Justin was hard-pressed to take what Rafe said seriously. But as the months progressed, and Jasmine grew more clingy, more demanding and more of what he was *not* looking or ready for, he was forced to tell Jasmine where they stood.

"Dinner is served." Bailey placed his meal in front of him.

Justin glanced up from the warm amber liquid of his glass only to swim in the depths of her chocolate-brown eyes. A slow heat flowed through his limbs. "Looks good. Thank you."

"Can I get you anything else?"

"Not at the moment."

"Enjoy." She started to walk away.

"Hey, uh, Bailey…"

She stopped and turned back to him. Her brows rose in question.

"How long does this place stay open?"

"Last call is at one. We close at two."

He nodded. "Is that when you get off? Two?"

"Yes. Late shift."

"Then what?"

She tilted her head. "Then what?"

"What do you do after you get off?"

"I'm usually too tired to do much more than go home… and go to bed." She swallowed.

He forked some risotto.

The smooth crooning sound of Kem's "A Matter of Time," moved languidly through the sound system. "Do you get a break in between?"

"Usually…when things slow down."

He nodded again without taking his eyes off her. "Stop by and check on me when you do."

"I can do that."

He lifted the fork to his mouth. "Looking forward."

Justin put the food in his mouth, chewed slowly, and unthinkable images of his mouth on her body ran havoc through her head.

Bailey inhaled deeply. "Enjoy your meal." She hurried away and told Mellie that she needed to run to the ladies' room.

Once in the privacy of the employee restroom, Bailey closed her eyes. She was actually shaking inside. It was obvious that Justin was making a play for her. She knew the signs and normally she was able to fend them off with a joke or another drink or deflect it with banal conversation. All of her tactics escaped her. She felt as if she'd been sucked in quicksand and couldn't grab on to anything to pull herself free. The music floated into the restroom.

Damn, damn, damn. She turned on the faucets and splashed cold water on her face and neck, snatched up a paper towel and dabbed the water away. She stared at her reflection. *Get it together, girl.* She sucked in a breath of determination and returned to her station.

Justin tried to concentrate on his meal, but his thoughts kept drifting back to Bailey. He could have been eating cardboard because he was only going through the motions. He wasn't sure what it was about her that had him thinking things he shouldn't be thinking. She was pretty. No doubt about that. But he'd seen and been with plenty of pretty women. That wasn't it. It was something that seeped from her pores and wrapped around him like a longed-for hug. It held him, soothed him and yes, excited him. She wasn't working him like so many of the women that he ran across. She had no idea who he was, who his family was. He wanted to keep it that way. He wanted— no *needed*—to find out what she was about, and maybe that discovery would answer the question that was hovering on the edge of his consciousness. Was she *the one*?

* * *

The evening moved on. The dance floor filled and emp-tied. The soft lighting tucked away in hidden places in the floor and pillars offered a seductive ambiance that was not lost on the patrons. Heads and bodies leaned close. Bubbles of laughter mixed with the music. Drinks flowed. Food satisfied the hungry palates. And Justin and Bailey teased and talked.

"So how long have you been working here?"

Bailey leaned her hip against the bar. "Going on three years."

"You must like it."

She smiled. His belly stirred.

"I do. You meet a lot of interesting people."

"Rumor has it that bartenders and hairdressers are like going to a confessional." His eyes caught the light and gleamed.

Bailey tossed her head back and laughed. Justin memo-rized the long curve of her throat.

"So I've heard. What about you? What do you do?"

He gauged his answer. "Attorney."

Her brows rose. "Really?"

"Is that a bad thing?"

"Not at all. Actually, I'm working on getting back into law school."

He rested his forearms on the counter. "Getting back?"

She lowered her gaze. "I had to drop out for a while."

"Oh." He nodded his head. "It can be hard." He paused. "Do you know what kind of law you want to practice?"

"I know that I don't want to work for a big corporate firm. My passion is to work with those wrongly accused and that don't have the means for high-priced attorneys. I'm thinking the nonprofit sector." She watched his ex-pression and was pleased that he didn't seem turned off by her altruistic vision.

"The business can certainly use more lawyers like you will be one day." He reached for his drink.

"I hope so. What about you? What kind of law do you practice?"

He smiled. "The kind that you don't want to be involved with, unfortunately."

"Why do you say *unfortunately*?"

"I'll put it this way. Sometimes we have to do things we don't necessarily want to in order to get where we want to go."

Bailey nodded.

"Tell me about law school Where did you go?"

"LSU."

He hummed approval deep in his throat. He sipped his drink. "Good school. Is that where you'll be in the fall?"

Bailey averted her gaze. "That's the plan."

Justin tried to reconcile her upbeat voice with her troubled expression—and couldn't. He wanted to ask her what was really going on, but he had experience with reluctant clients. It was clear that she was hesitant and could have been for any number of reasons. What he also knew was that if asked the right questions and given enough space, a client would tell you everything you wanted to know.

"Law school, even under the best circumstances, is rough, especially if you have to take a semester off." He casually glanced at her.

Bailey's lips moved as if she would respond, but she didn't. He tried again.

"My second year my best friend Carl had to drop out— family issues. In solidarity I took off a semester, too. My family had a fit. But Carl and I made a pact when we started that we would enter together and leave together."

Her expression softened. "A man of your word."

"I try to be."

She offered a tight smile. "I better get back to work. Can I get you anything else?"

"No. I'm good. Just the check."

She nodded. "Be right back." Once he had his check there would be no reason for him to stay. She could only stall for so long. What if she didn't see him again? Why was it even important if she did? She punched in the information for his bill. There was a solidness about Justin, a confidence and warmth that couldn't be manufactured. She stole a look in his direction. She wanted to get to know him, and she knew deep in her soul that he was feeling the same vibe.

"Here's your check." She placed the bill in front of him.

He took a look at the bill. If he paid with his credit card, she'd know who he was. He wasn't ready to cross that line yet. He wanted to get to know her on his terms without the distraction of the Lawson name. Bailey seemed down to earth, a regular woman with a good head on her shoulders, but they all did in the beginning. He needed to give this some time. He plucked his wallet from his inside jacket pocket and took out a fifty and a twenty.

"I'll bring your change."

"Keep it."

Her brows flicked. "Thanks."

"Sure," he said quietly.

Justin pushed back and stood. "How many nights are you here?" he asked.

She blinked. "Oh, um, most nights, except Sunday and one Saturday a month."

"In that case, I'll see you again. If that's okay."

"Sure. I'd like that."

He gave her the full benefit of his smile that caused the lights to dance in her eyes. "See you soon, Bailey."

"Take care." He walked around the tables to the front and out the door. And for whatever crazy reason, he already missed her smile.

Chapter 3

Bailey chopped a bushel of collard greens while Addison seasoned a tub of crawfish. Addison had a bachelor party that she was catering for on the weekend, and there was still fish to fry and sticky rice to make.

"So, he was cute, huh?" Addison asked.

"More than cute."

"Did you give him your number?"

"Of course not." She paused. "He didn't ask, but he did say he wanted to see me again."

"That's a start. What does he do?"

"Lawyer."

"Jackpot!"

Bailey laughed. "You would say that."

"Well, it's true, but what's more important is that you actually took an interest in somebody." She glanced at Bailey from the corner of her eye. "It's been a long time since Adam. All you do is work and take care of your selfish family. When is it going to be your time?"

"Addy, don't start."

Addison stopped with her seasoning and propped her hand on her hip. "You know it's true, B. Your sisters drain the life out of you. You have bills up the you know what and no daylight in sight. You need someone—for you. Maybe this guy is it."

"I'm not looking for some man to take care of me, Addy. I *won't* be my mother." Her features tightened.

Addison flinched. Men. Money. Mom. The three *M*s

that remained a bone of contention for Bailey, and no amount of prodding or coaxing had changed any of it. She pushed out a breath of apology. "Sorry. I don't mean to… I just know how hard things can be for you. How hard they are." She reached out and touched Bailey's arm. "I'm your girl, Bailey. I only want you to be happy. That's all."

Bailey lowered her gaze. "I know," she murmured. She slowly shook her head. "Did I tell you that Tory called?"

"How much did she want this time?"

"Twelve hundred."

"What! Bailey…"

Bailey held up her hand. "Don't say it, okay? I know."

"Tory has got to stand on her own two feet, and she never will if you keep bailing her out."

Bailey spun toward Addison. "She's my sister. I can't just…" She covered her face with her hands.

Addison came to her side and put her arm around her shoulder. "Sweetie, when it's not Tory it's Apryl with her man-crazy self. You can't continue to carry them on your shoulders. They're living their lives. When are you going to live yours? What about going back to law school? How are you going to manage that if you keep…" She blew out a breath of utter frustration.

"I made a promise to myself when my mother died. I promised that I would look after my sisters."

"And that's what you've been doing. You put your entire life on hold, dropped out of school, worked like a field hand to take care of them and pick up their broken pieces over and over. It's your time, damn it!" She slapped down the towel on the counter.

"I don't want to talk about this anymore." She focused on the sink full of greens, wishing that it would turn into dollars and make all her troubles go away. But money wasn't the answer. Her mother was proof of that. But what Addison said was true. She knew that, as well. She *did* want someone in her life, someone to take care of her for a change, make her feel wanted, needed and loved. If she was waiting on that from her family, she knew she'd be waiting a very long time.

"What's next?" Bailey asked, shaking the water off the greens and putting them in a giant pot of seasoned steaming water.

Addison looked at her friend and saw the resolute expression in the tight line of her mouth and knew that the subject of Bailey and her family drama was closed.

"The fish needs to be dredged in the seasoning."

"Got it."

They worked in silence for a while; the only sound was the boiling water and busy hands.

"I hope he comes back again," Bailey said in a near whisper. She slid a glance in Addison's direction.

Addison grinned. "She lives!"

Every night for the next two weeks Bailey went to work with the hopes of seeing Justin again. Each night ended in disappointment.

He wasn't coming back. He talked a good game and that was it. What would a high-priced lawyer want with a bartender/would-be law student? This was why she didn't get involved, didn't hope for anything more than light conversation to pass the time. If you didn't expect anything, you couldn't be fooled or disappointed. But he'd seemed genuinely interested in her. It was probably her own need that she thought she saw reflected in him. Nothing more. He was no different from Adam. She pressed her hand to her stomach. No different.

"Hey, Bailey, it's Addy."

Bailey smiled. "Like you really have to tell me who you are. How long have we known each other—third grade?" She curved her body into the contours of her armchair and draped her leg across the arm.

"Must I remind you *not* to remind me how long we've known each other? It's much too long, and we couldn't possibly be as old as that third grade friendship would make us."

Bailey snickered. "Whatever, girl." She rested the novel that she'd been reading on her lap, and actually turned it facedown as if Addison could see that she was reading the steamy scene of a romance novel. "Whats up?"

"I'm in a jam."

Bailey shifted her position. Her senses went on alert. Addison was the most together person she knew. If Addy was in a jam, what hope did she have? "A jam. What's wrong? Are you okay?"

"Yes. I'm fine. Relax. I'm in a jam because I have a mega big party to cater this weekend, and I'm short staffed. One of my bartenders has the flu, and a hostess is preggers. So I'm crossing my eyes, my fingers and toes that you're free this weekend to help out. Pretty please."

"Addy, you don't have to ask twice. As strapped as I am for cash—I'll be there. What day, time and where?"

"Saturday night. I need you at least by seven. Can you swing that with Vince?"

"I'll make it work. I'll do the early shift. Where is this shindig?"

"At the Lawson mansion. They are throwing an 85th birthday party for the family patriarch. The guest list is loaded with Louisiana's who's who, athletes, television and movie stars, the works. So I know tips are going to be off the charts."

"*The* Lawsons…the father is Senator Lawson, right?"

"Yes."

"You done made it to the big time, girl. Count me in."

Addison breathed a sigh of relief. "Thanks. I'll text you the address. Maybe if we get lucky we'll land us a rich ballplayer or something."

"Whatever," she chuckled. "See you Saturday. And don't forget to text me the info."

"Will do. Thanks again."

"Not a problem." Bailey disconnected the call, feeling a bit brighter in spirit. She could use every extra penny, so this job could not have come along at a better time. She picked up her novel and dived in with gusto. At least she could live vicariously through the love lives of the characters.

Surprisingly, Vincent had given her a bit of a hard time when she told him she would be switching shifts. They'd actually had a real back and forth until he finally conceded. It was so unlike him, at least with her. She knew he was overworked, but she carried her end and more. It had to be something else. Their little verbal sparring was days earlier and even though he'd said everything was fine, he remained distant with her, barely looking at her when he did speak, and then his conversation was minimal at best.

Well, whatever mood he was in, he would get over it, she thought as she hustled out of the Mercury Lounge to run home and change. The Lawson mansion was at the edge of the parish where the plantations once dominated the landscape. It would take her at least a half hour to get there from her house barring any Saturday night traffic.

When she finally pulled onto the street where the mansion was located, her eyes widened in awe. The sprawling lawn that had to be several acres in size was dotted with white tents that protected circular tables covered in white linen and topped with purple orchids. Red-vested valets were busy parking the cars that had already begun to arrive. Twinkling lights were strung through the overhanging trees that gave the entire space a fairy-tale feel. Soft music came from some unseen source and wafted across the warm night air.

Wow was all she could manage as a valet came to park

her car after asking if she had an invitation. She could not imagine herself being invited to a place like this. Working here, maybe, but invited… It was so out of touch with her reality.

She turned over her keys, gathered her belongings and walked up the slight incline to the main entrance. If she thought only the outside was fabulous, she was sadly mistaken. The interior of the Lawson mansion was clearly out of some designer's dream. It had the influence of the antebellum age with all of the modern twists. Stunning chandeliers spewed diamond-like light across the gleaming wood floors. The winding staircase looked as if it could lead to heaven and beyond. Long tables lined the walls on three sides, covered from end to end with silver-covered platters. There was a small raised landing set up for a band that was tuning up their instruments. Two bars were on either side of the room with an additional bar on the patio. The wide-open layout added to the feeling of spaciousness that allowed for a magnificent view of the entire ground floor. The back wall was all glass and opened onto an amazing deck and more acreage, a pool and additional outside seating.

The house was buzzing with staff, and the heady aroma of food momentarily made her dizzy when she realized that she hadn't eaten since lunchtime.

"There you are! I was getting worried." Addison grabbed Bailey by the arm. "They're keeping the guests outside for the time being. Girl, I might be in over my head."

Bailey glanced at Addison and actually saw panic in her eyes. "Why, what's wrong?"

She lowered her voice. "I've never done anything this big or this important before. Suppose something goes wrong?"

Bailey squeezed Addison's hand and looked her straight in the eye. "They're just people who want to have a good time. You are a kick-ass caterer with an amazing staff and…you got me." She grinned, and the tight line between Addison's eyes softened.

Addison released a breath. "That's what I needed to hear."

"Good. Now, where do you want me?"

Within the hour, the front doors were opened for the guests, and the party was in full swing.

Bailey mixed a martini and handed it to the quarterback for the New Orleans Saints, followed by a gin and tonic for the morning show host for the NBC affiliate. Addison was right about the guest list. In the short time since the doors opened, Bailey had spotted several familiar faces from reality television, not to mention two Oscar winners. Addison was also right about the amount of work. They could barely keep up at the bar. She shifted her duties from one side of the room to the other and also supervised the bar outside. That didn't include keeping up with refilling the flutes of champagne that the waiters carried on trays. Rich folks sure could drink.

She had yet to spot the guest of honor, but she did get a glimpse at a few of the Lawson clan that was pointed out to her by one of the other bartenders. They were certainly a good-looking family. What did it take to be this wealthy, to be on a first-name basis with people that she only read about? This was so not her world.

The steady hum of voices and trilling laughter mixed with the four-piece combo that had taken the stage. Couples bejeweled and bedecked made their way to the dance floor while others continued to mingle and network, eat and drink.

She looked up to take yet another order and stopped cold. *It was Justin.* He was heart-stopping in his tailored black tie ensemble. She couldn't breathe. He was walking right in her direction with a stunning woman glued to his arm. What was he doing here? Her heart hammered, and she accidentally splashed vodka on the counter instead of in the glass. She quickly got a damp cloth to clean up the spill just as Justin and his date approached.

"Bailey?"

She shoved the rag under the bar. Her gaze jumped from his surprised expression to the cover model face of his date that looked more annoyed than anything else.

"What can I get you?"

"I had no idea…"

"I'll have a cosmopolitan," his date said, cutting him off.

Justin shot her a sharp look. Her brows arched as if to ask *what*?

Bailey got busy making the drink. Her hands shook.

"How have you been?"

"Fine," she murmured. She finished the drink and placed it in front of his date.

"You're chummy with the help now? That's so like you, Justin." She lifted her drink to her polished, plump lips.

"Jasmine!" he snapped.

Bailey was mortified.

He was about to say something to Bailey when a richly accented Louisiana drawl voice came over the microphone.

"Can I have everyone's attention?"

By degrees the room quieted.

"I want to welcome each of you to my home to celebrate the 85th birthday of my father, Clive Lawson."

There was a rousing round of applause.

Branford Lawson gazed out at the throng, clearly comfortable addressing a crowd. "Before we continue with the festivities, I want the members of the family to come on up."

Jasmine tugged on Justin's arm. Justin threw a look at Bailey from over his shoulder and mouthed, "I'm sorry," before walking away.

"First I want to introduce the family of Clive Lawson,"

Branford announced. "My sister, Jacqueline, my uncles Paul and Jake Lawson, their offspring Craig, Miles, Alyse, Sydni, Devon and Conner and my brother David's son, Maurice."

One by one they each stepped up onto the platform, one more gorgeous than the next.

"And my brood—my eldest Rafe, my daughters Lee Ann, Desiree and Dominique and last but surely not least, my youngest son, Justin."

Bailey's mouth dropped open. *Justin was a Lawson.* Her temples began to pound.

"My father and my mother, Sylvia, God rest her soul, made all of this possible. He set the foundation for the Lawson family, and I hope that we have made and will continue to make him proud by carrying on the great tradition of the Lawson family. Happy birthday, Dad." Branford raised his glass as did all of the guests as Clive Lawson slowly made his way to the front of his family.

Clive Lawson, even at eighty-five, was a powerfully built man. He still had a head full of snow-white hair, and the hard lines etched in his deep brown face told of his years of intense work and struggle, but the sparkle in his eyes told the real story. Pride.

Branford handed the microphone to Jacqueline, who passed it to her father.

Clive took in the eager faces. "Thank ya'll for coming. I 'preciate it." He nodded his head while he formed the words. "A man's family is his legacy, and I couldn't be more proud of mine." He glanced behind him and smiled at his assembled family. "I know I can't be here forever, but when I do leave, I know that I've done all I could. All I've ever asked is that my children and their children be true to themselves and make things better for the next. Thank ya'll again. Now, let's party!"

The room erupted in cheers and applause as the family stepped away from the stage, and the guests swarmed around Clive to wish him congratulations.

Addison appeared next to Bailey. "Big family, huh?"

Bailey was still in stunned silence.

Addison nudged her with her elbow. "Hey, you okay?"

"It's him."

"Him who?"

"Justin. The Justin that I told you about."

Addison's eyes widened. "Say what? *Your* Justin is *the* Justin Lawson?"

Bailey numbly nodded her head. "Yeah, *the* Justin Lawson."

Chapter 4

For the rest of the evening Bailey performed by rote, going through the motions and keeping a painted smile on her face, but her mind was elsewhere. She periodically scanned the room for a glimpse of Justin, but at the same time she didn't want to see him. His date's comment about talking to the help still stung, and it certainly made her question his choice of companions. What was clear was that this was not her life. It was so far removed from her reality. The rooms reeked of money and power. And Justin was part of it.

It was nearing 2:00 a.m., and the crowd had finally wound down. Addison was still in nonstop motion, checking on every detail that was under her supervision. She worked with drill-sergeant efficiency in getting her staff to wrap up the festivities, clean up, pack supplies and load them onto the rented vans.

"Whew, what a night," Addison huffed as she leaned against the counter. "We did it, and thank you so much for pitching in."

"No problem," Bailey murmured as she stacked glasses in boxes.

"You okay?"

"Fine. Just tired, that's all."

Addison studied her friend's contemplative profile. "It's more than being tired. What's up? Is it about Justin Lawson and that *woman*?"

Inside she flinched. "No. Of course not. I was surprised to see him here, that's all."

"And…?"

"And nothing." She kept her gaze averted.

"Did you talk to him?"

"No. Why would I?"

"Because the few times that I did get a glimpse of him, he was looking in your direction, but his date was holding on to him like he was pumping air into her lungs."

Bailey couldn't help but snicker. "That she was. It doesn't matter. If I even thought for a minute that there was any possibility for us to see each other, that went out the window tonight."

"Why, because of that chick?"

"Mainly…and…just look at this place, the people who were here tonight. They come from a completely different place than me."

Addison pushed out a sigh. "Girl, you don't give yourself enough credit. Take off the diamonds and that designer gown, and you have the woman beat hands down."

Bailey turned to Addison with a slight smirk. "You have to say that because you love me."

"Yeah, but it doesn't make what I said any less true."

By the time Bailey pulled into her parking spot, it was almost four in the morning. She was bone tired. All she wanted to do was take a hot bath, get into her bed and sleep for two days. Thankfully, she wasn't on duty until seven that evening, and she intended to spend every minute of it off her feet.

The Mercury Lounge was already busy by the time Bailey arrived. Although there wasn't a waiting list for tables, she knew that wouldn't last long. She waved hello to her coworkers and walked through the space to her back office. She quickly reviewed the roster for the evening and verified the schedule. Satisfied that the lounge was fully staffed for the current shift and the following day, she changed clothes to her standard black blouse and slacks and headed out front. Vincent was off tonight, so she had double duty to manage the bar as well as run the restaurant. She did a quick walk-through on each of the levels, chatted briefly with the staff and floor managers and visited the kitchen to check in with the chef. Thankfully, there were no private parties going on tonight that she had to worry about. All systems go.

Addison had promised to drop in later on and hang out for a while to chat. She was looking forward to seeing her friend. They hadn't had a chance to catch up and gossip since the party. *The party.* A twinge tightened her stomach. She still had a hard time believing how it all went down with Justin. First to find out that the man she'd been fantasizing about was a member of one of the most wealthy and powerful families in the state of Louisiana. Second, he was clearly involved with someone else. She shook her head in resignation. It was a nice fantasy while it lasted. She tied the apron around her waist and went to work. Soon she was fully involved in chatting up the customers and mixing drinks. And then there he was, coming through the front door, and she wanted to go through the floor.

Justin spotted Bailey right away and strode purposefully in her direction. Her feet felt glued to the ground.

"Hey." He slid onto the bar stool.

"Hi. What can I get you?" She refused to engage in eye contact.

"Jim Beam. No ice."

She gave a brief nod and turned to the row of bottles behind her.

"Ohhh, I see Mr. Fine is back," Mellie said, sidling up to Bailey.

"Yep," she said noncommittally. She reached for the bottle and nearly dropped it because her hands were shaking so badly. She managed to fix the drink and place it in front of him.

"Here you go. Anything else, let me know." She started to turn away, and Justin grabbed her hand.

"Wait."

She glanced down at his hand covering hers. Electricity skidded up her arm. Her lips parted slightly so that she could breathe.

"I want to apologize about the other night."

"Nothing to apologize for."

"Yes, there is. Jasmine was rude, and her comment was uncalled for. I don't want you to think that's how I think or what I feel."

She blinked. Her thoughts scrambled. She swallowed. "Whatever."

"It's true."

Her heart was beating a mile a minute. If he didn't let go of her hand, she would self-combust. She pulled her hand away. "Thanks for the apology. I've got to get back to work."

"And I'll be right here until you talk to me."

She threw him a look, and he stared right back at her. On shaky legs she turned away and walked to the end of the bar.

"What's the deal with Mr. Handsome?" Mellie asked. "I saw him grab your hand. Girl, you need to stop playing so hard to get. Even Stevie Wonder could see he has a thing for you."

"Mellie, would you please stop? He does not."

"Hmm, okay. If you say so."

Bailey dared to glance down the length of the bar, and Justin raised his glass to her. She quickly looked away. Was he really going to sit there all night? And where in the hell was Addison?

Bailey's cell phone chirped in her pocket. She pulled it

out and saw Addy's name on the screen. "Girl, where are you?" she asked under her breath.

"I'm running a little late. What's wrong?"

"He's here."

"Who?"

"Him. Justin."

"Oh, damn. Well, what happened?"

"Nothing. He said he came to apologize."

"Okay, and…"

"And, I can't talk to that man, and he said he's staying until I do."

"Don't be ridiculous. Obviously, he's interested. He didn't have to come to see you."

"He also is obviously involved."

"Maybe, maybe not. You'll never find out talking to me. See you soon."

Bailey heaved a sigh and stuck the phone back into her pocket. She glanced at Justin, who was nursing his drink. She straightened her shoulders and walked back down the length of the bar and stood in front of him.

"I accept your apology."

He looked at her from beneath those incredible lashes. He set his drink down. "Good. That's a start."

"A start to what?"

"To us getting to know each other."

"What about…your friend…Jasmine?"

"It's not what you think."

"How do you know what I'm thinking?"

"You're thinking that she and I have a real thing going on. That she's my woman and therefore there is no room for an us."

Her stomach fluttered at the tone of his word *us*. "There isn't an us."

"There can be. If you give me a chance to show you."

"You still haven't answered my question about you and Jasmine."

"Ask. What do you want to know? I have nothing to hide."

Her gaze darted around then finally settled on him. "What…how serious is it between you?" She ran her tongue across her bottom lip.

Justin angled his head to the side. "She is the daughter of one of the partners at the firm where I work. Her father and mine think that the two of us would make a perfect partnership." He paused, looked beyond her defenses and seeped down into her center. "I don't." He slowly turned his glass on the bar top, studying the remnants of the amber liquid. He lifted his dark eyes. "I want to get to know you."

Her heart thudded, and her flesh heated. The sound of his voice, the look of raw hunger in his eyes, had her wanting to believe whatever those luscious lips said.

She rested her weight on her right leg. "You used to getting what you want, Mr. Lawson?"

"Most of the time. But I do go after what I want…all the time."

Her nipples tightened. She tore her gaze away. "We come from two different worlds. I'm not the kind of woman you're used to."

"How can you be so sure that you know what I'm used to…better, what I want?"

"I was at the party, remember? I saw the kind of circles you travel in."

"And you think that's all I am?"

"Aren't you?" she challenged.

"No. And I want to prove that to you."

"Why? Why me?"

He hesitated. "Because I can't stop thinking about you. Day and night. I want to know what it's like to kiss those lips of yours, to hold you, touch you, to whisper in your ear, to make love to you." He ran the tip of his finger along her knuckles.

Her skin sizzled, and her clit twitched in response.

"I've got to get back to work," she managed to eek out.

"I'll be here when you get a break."

And he was true to his word. Justin ordered dinner at the bar. And each time that she came in his direction, he made a joke, or shared something about himself, like how he painted in his spare time, that one of his favorite vacation spots was Sag Harbor in the summer, and that his older brother, Rafe, was one of his best friends. And Bailey laughed at his corny jokes and told him about her best friend, Addison, and how she helped her out from time to time. She told him that she really enjoyed her job and how much she wanted to get back to law school.

"You mentioned that the last time we talked. Law school. Maybe I could help."

She stopped short. "What do you mean *help*?" she said a bit more harsh than necessary.

He held up his hands in surrender. "Whoa. All I meant was that maybe I could make a few calls."

"No! If I get in, it will be on my own, not because some big shot pulled some strings." She spun away, fuming on the inside. How dare he? But what could she expect? Clearly he saw her as some poor waif who needed rescuing by a knight in shining armor.

"Hey, girl!"

Bailey turned around. "It's about time," she groused.

"What is wrong with you?"

"Nothing."

Addison looked around and noticed Justin at the end of the bar. "Something go wrong?"

"Yeah, plenty. Be right back. We need some clean glasses." She stormed off.

Addison eased down the bar and took a seat that became vacant next to Justin.

"Justin Lawson, right?"

"Yes." He offered her a heart-stopping smile. His eyes cinched as he stared at her. "You're the caterer."

She grinned. "Good memory, especially with all the people there that night."

He chuckled. "I try to remember faces."

She extended her hand. "Addison Matthews."

"Pleasure." He reached for his drink and took a sip. "So you're Bailey's friend."

"Best friend."

"Hmm. Best friend." He glanced in Bailey's direction, and she was trying hard not to look interested.

"She's hard to get to know."

"Not really. She's cautious, that's all."

He nodded. "Any suggestions?"

"About?"

"About how to get past all of her caution signs."

Addison rested her forearms on the counter. She faced him. "Be honest. Bailey is a wonderful woman who puts everyone and everything ahead of herself. She could use someone in her life that puts her first for a change." She offered a tight smile and slid off the stool. "Nice to meet you, Mr. Lawson."

"Justin."

Addison glanced over her shoulder. "Justin."

By the time Bailey returned with the rack of clean glasses, Addison was already in deep conversation with a guy who'd taken a seat next to her.

Bailey unloaded the glasses. Things were always so easy for Addison when it came to men. She was fearless. She didn't care what anyone thought, and she went after who and what she wanted. There were times when she wished that she could be as cavalier about relationships; just get in them for the good times and move on. But she couldn't. She wanted more than the momentary excitement. She wanted something that would last and someone that would make *her* a priority—for once. If there was one thing that Addy was right about, it was that she did need someone to take care of her for a change. Some days she simply wanted to get in her car and drive and keep on going. But she couldn't. Her family depended on her. She finished stacking the glasses on the shelf and hanging them from the overhead rack, and when she turned around, Justin was standing in front of her.

"Wanted to say good night and pay my tab."

A knot formed in her stomach. *He was leaving.* What if he didn't come back? "Sure. I'll put your bill together." She swung toward the register. Her heart thumped, and her hands shook. The register spewed out his bill. She handed it to him.

Justin barely glanced at it. He reached in his jacket pocket and took out his wallet and handed her his black American Express card.

Bailey numbly processed the payment and returned his card. "Have a good evening," she managed to say.

Justin stared at her for a moment. A slow smile moved his mouth. "Hope to see you again when I come back."

She smiled in return. "I'd like that."

Justin took a step back. "Night."

"Night."

He was coming back, and he wanted to see her. Bailey held on to that promise.

Chapter 5

For the next two weeks, Justin, true to his word, showed up at the Mercury Lounge at least three nights a week. Bailey quietly looked forward to seeing him, although she never told him as much. When he walked through the doors and took what had become his usual seat, all the lights came on in her world, and she sailed through the night.

On the evenings that Justin didn't show up, Bailey experienced an incredible emptiness, a malaise almost as if she was lifting her feet in and out of mud.

Tonight was one of those nights. Every time the door swung open, her heart leaped only to stutter in her chest when it wasn't him.

Bailey wiped down the bar top and began putting away bottles and stacking glasses for washing. Tonight made two nights in a row that Justin had not made an appearance.

He had probably gone back to his fancy life, which was fine with her. She was crazy to think that he was really interested in her beyond some casual conversation to pass the time.

Justin was in the thick of preparing a case for one of the partners where he would serve as second chair, but his thoughts kept drifting back to the night of the party and seeing Bailey. He'd wanted to see her again, but the past couple of weeks had been grueling with him clocking in twelve-hour days. But he knew that when he saw her again, he had to come right. And coming right meant dealing with the futility of his relationship with Jasmine DuBois. As if he'd talked her up, his phone rang and it was Jasmine.

"Justin Lawson."

"Hey, sweetie."

Justin put down his pen. "Hey, Jasmine. I'm really busy right now—"

"I know. That's why I'm calling. You've been working nonstop, and don't think for a moment that Daddy hasn't noticed."

Justin's jaw tightened.

"Anyway, sweetie, I made reservations for dinner tonight. You deserve it, and it will give us a chance to talk about us."

Justin ran his hand across his face. "Jazz, I told you before, we can only be friends…a serious relationship won't work for us."

"If you're worried about what Daddy is going to say, I can handle him," she said, oblivious to what was really being said to her.

If he ever doubted for a minute before that this relationship with Jasmine was a disaster in the making, all of his doubts vanished. Jasmine's selfish single-mindedness was impenetrable. All she saw and all she wanted was whatever it took to satisfy her desires. The needs and aspirations of others never entered her radar. In the beginning, he felt that her superficiality was all for show, and that once they got to know each other, she would allow him to see the real her—a woman with some substance. He was still waiting. He wouldn't wait any longer.

"What time are the reservations and where?"

Jasmine giddily gave him the information.

"I'll meet you there."

"Sure. See you at seven…" She giggled.

"I've got to go, Jazz."

"Sure, sweetie. See you tonight."

Justin arrived home and was surprised to see his eldest sister, LeeAnn, tinkering around in the kitchen.

"Lee!" He dropped his briefcase at the entrance to the kitchen. "What are you doing here?"

LeeAnn turned from peering into the fridge and beamed a smile of delight in seeing her brother. She shut the door and crossed the room. "Hi, baby bro." She reached up and kissed his cheek. He held her hand.

"Long way from your new home in DC. Preston here, too?"

"He should be soon."

Justin frowned. "Everything okay?"

"Actually, everything's great. Desi and Dominique are going to come by also."

"Desi and Dom? Okay, spill it. What's really going on?" He leaned against the island counter.

LeeAnn drew in a breath. "Well, I wanted everyone here so that we'd only have to say it once, but I guess I can tell you if you swear you won't say anything until the rest of the family gets here."

He ran his finger across his lips in a zipper motion.

But before LeeAnn could say a word they heard the front door and the near identical voices of Desiree and Dominique in animated conversation.

"Hello, good people," Dominique greeted as she entered the archway. She kissed her brother and sister.

"What's all the secrecy, sis?" Desiree asked. She placed her purse on the counter and hugged LeeAnn then Justin.

"Yeah, spill the tea, girl," Dominique said.

LeeAnn grinned. "Can we wait for my husband to get here?"

"Well, I don't know about y'all, but I'm starving," Dominique groused. She headed to the fridge and pulled the door open then plucked out an apple. "Are you at least fixing dinner, Lee, since you got us all over here?"

LeeAnn had always been the great cook of the family, and they'd all come to expect her to whip up one of her special dishes whenever she was home. Being the eldest girl, she'd all but taken over caring for her siblings after they'd lost their mother, Louisa, and they all still looked to her for all the things that a mother would do.

"I hadn't planned to, but I suppose I could put something together."

Justin checked his watch. Jasmine was expecting him in an hour. The evening was going to be tough enough. He didn't want to add being late to the mix. But, family first. Jasmine would have to understand. "I need to make a call." He excused himself and walked into the front room. He pulled out his phone and called Jasmine.

The phone barely rang before Jasmine picked up.

"Hello, Justin," she said.

"Hi. Listen, something came up here at the house. I'm going to be late getting to you."

Silence.

"Jazz?"

"Fine. What's late?"

"I don't know, but I'll call you when I'm done here."

"We have reservations," she whined.

Justin's jaw tightened. "I know that."

He heard her blow an exasperated breath into the phone. "Well, we can cancel, and you can come here."

That was the last thing he wanted to do, but he also had no intention of dragging out the inevitable. "Sure. I'll see you as soon as I can."

"I'll make it worth your while," she cooed.

"See you later." He disconnected the call, stuck his phone back into his pocket and returned to the family gathered in the kitchen.

"Everything okay?" Dominique quietly asked while she sipped on a glass of wine.

"Yeah." He reached for the bottle of wine and filled his own glass. Of his three sisters, it was Dominique that could always read him. There was a closeness between them that often rivaled the relationship between her and her twin, Desiree. Dominique was the wild one, or so most people thought. But underneath her diva exterior, she was insightful, caring and wise beyond her years. Meanwhile, it was Desi that had a passion for the dangerous world of race-car driving. When that little tidbit of information got to their father, he nearly imploded.

LeeAnn and Desiree were busy catching up and preparing dinner for the clan. Dominique slid her arm around her brother's waist and peeked up at him above the rim of her glass. "What's really going on?"

"With LeeAnn? I know what you know. Nada." He gave a half grin.

"You know that's not what I mean." She gently nudged him in the side with her elbow. "What's going on with you? I know that look."

"You mean my strong jaw and charismatic smile." He chuckled lightly and stroked his smooth chin.

"Don't play with me."

He blew out a breath. "Making some moves, that's all."

She arched a questioning brow. "That's your final answer?"

He angled his body away from LeeAnn and Desiree to face Dominique. "Working out some things with Jasmine. She needs to understand where we stand."

"How is that going to affect things at the office?"

He gave a half shrug. "We'll see."

"If it helps, I think you're making the right decision. Jasmine is a woman for someone else. She's all about Jasmine and getting ahead and latching on to name and money." She clasped his upper biceps. "You have a vision, ambition and a commitment to society. I can't see Jasmine ever being a part of that."

Justin slowly nodded. "I agree. Don't get me wrong. I care about her. Beneath all of the shine of her exterior, she's trying to find her way. But she has been so spoiled by the life her parents have provided for her that she has no empathy for anyone who she believes has less than her. That's a big problem for me. I tried to ignore it and hoped that it was just a facade, but it's at the heart of who she is." He slowly shook his head. "I know I'm not the one for her."

"It'll be fine. Was that who you were calling?"

"Yeah. We had reservations for dinner. I'd planned to talk to her at the restaurant. Unfortunately, I didn't anticipate this…" He gave a slight tilt of his head toward his sisters.

"Hmm. So what *are* you going to do?"

"Meet at her place when we're done here."

"You know I got you covered if you need a ride-along," she teased.

Justin chuckled. "Thanks, but no need. I'm good."

"Well, I'm just a cell phone call away." She winked and sauntered over to her sisters just as the doorbell rang.

LeeAnn wiped her hands on a paper towel. "That should be Preston." She walked out and went to the front door.

"I hope so. Then we can get this party started," Dominique said and refilled her glass of wine.

Moments later LeeAnn and Preston walked in arm in arm, with LeeAnn beaming at her husband like the day she married him.

"The gang's all here," Preston greeted, kissing the cheeks of his sisters-in-law and shaking Justin's hand.

"Everyone but Rafe," Desiree added.

"I'd hoped that he would be able to make it, but he has a gig in South Beach tonight at the Versace mansion," LeeAnn said.

"He does get around," Preston said with an air of admiration.

"All this small talk is nice, but will somebody please tell me what the hell is going on so we can eat?" Dominique said.

LeeAnn looked up at her husband, and he shared a "go ahead" nod.

"Well…we have news on a couple of fronts." She drew in a breath and pushed out what they were waiting to hear. "We're pregnant."

"I knew it!" Desiree screeched.

"Congratulations, y'all," Dominique added.

"Congrats, sis and you, too, Preston," Justin joked.

They all shared hugs and kisses, and when the excitement died down to murmurs of happiness for the couple, LeeAnn took Preston's hand. "There's more."

The room quieted.

"I was offered a position with the Department of State as Deputy Director of Environmental Policy Implementation," Preston said.

A chorus of congratulations filled the air.

"Thanks. It's something that I've always wanted to do, and serving in the Senate on the environmental committee paved the way." He paused. "The position is in Kenya."

"Kenya…as in Africa, Kenya?" Desiree asked, her voice rising in pitch.

"We leave in three weeks," LeeAnn added.

Dominique put down her glass. "What? You're moving to Kenya?"

"That's a big move, brah," Justin said. "You both ready for that?" He looked from one to the other.

"We are," LeeAnn said.

"Hey, you have to do what you can to make a difference, and I know you will," Justin said. He stepped to his brother-in-law and gave him a hearty hug. "Proud of you, man."

"Thanks."

"How long will you be gone?" Desiree asked, her voice cracking.

"At least a year. It could be extended. But for now, it's a year."

"What about the baby? You're going to have the baby in Kenya?" Dominique asked, her dismay finally kicking in.

LeeAnn offered a tight smile. "Looks that way."

"Dad is going to have a natural fit," Desiree said.

"That's why we wanted to tell you all first, get your support," LeeAnn said. "You know Dad. He wants things his way, and he has Preston's entire career mapped out."

"You don't really think that Dad doesn't know, do you?" Justin said. "Nothing gets past him, and he's right there in the mix in DC."

"True. I'm sure he's heard the rumors, but he hasn't approached me, and I didn't want to say anything until LeeAnn and I had thoroughly talked about it. It's what we both want."

"You have my support," Justin said.

Desiree and Dominique added their words of support, as well, albeit a bit halfhearted.

"Damn, how in the world am I going to arrange a baby shower way the hell in Kenya?" Dominique said, and whatever thread of tension that was in the air was broken.

"I say this calls for a Lawson family toast," Desiree said then made sure everyone had a glass of wine except for LeeAnn, who had iced tea.

"To LeeAnn and Preston and the safe arrival of the newest Lawson-Graham," Justin said and raised his glass.

LeeAnn turned to Preston. "Think we should tell them the rest?"

"You do the honors, babe."

"Make that *two* little Lawson-Grahams. Doctor said it's twins." LeeAnn's eyes gleamed with joy.

Squeals and deep rumbles of shock and happy congratulations rippled through the expansive kitchen.

Justin was still smiling when he pulled out of the driveway en route to Jasmine's home on the far end of the parish. It takes real courage to make a major move like that,
especially being a relative newlywed and expecting twins,
he thought. Toss Branford Lawson into the mix, and it
could be a real mess. None of that was stopping Preston
from pushing ahead in the direction that he needed to go,
and LeeAnn was right there by his side. At a time when
most women would need to be around their family and
close friends, his sister was willing to forgo all of that to
support her husband. That was love.

He was more determined than ever to pursue his own
dream, and if he could be as lucky as Preston was in finding a treasure like his sister LeeAnn, the dream would be
that much sweeter.

Twenty minutes later he pulled up in front of Jasmine's
two-story home. He parked in the driveway behind Jasmine's candy-apple-red Porsche and stepped out into the
twinkling twilight of the late-spring evening. Hopefully,
Jasmine wouldn't make this any more difficult than it had
to be. He walked up the short lane that was braced on either side by emerald-green hedges, stopped at the front
door and rang the bell.

Jasmine opened the door moments later. There was
no denying that Jasmine DuBois was a stunning woman.
Wherever she went, heads turned, with men wanting to
know her and women wishing they were her. There was
a small corner of Justin's ego that enjoyed the fact that
she was on his arm. But as the old saying goes, beauty
is only skin deep. What Jasmine exuded on the outside
ended there. In the months of their dating, it had become
more and more apparent how shallow and self-absorbed
she really was.

"Hey, sweetie." She extended her slender hand and led him inside.

"Hey."

Justin closed the door behind him and before he could barely turn, Jasmine had wrapped herself around him, enveloped him in her kiss, pressed the curves of her body against his. It was clear what she wanted.

Justin clasped her upper arms and pulled away, holding her in place. Her eyes flashed. Her chest heaved.

"What's wrong? What is it?"

"You know what's wrong, Jazz. Us."

She tugged away as if she'd been slapped. "What are you talking about?"

Justin crossed the space into the front room and turned to face her. "We want two different things, Jasmine. The life you want to lead is not my life. There's so much more than the next social event, and island hopping and new clothes and cars. There are people out there hurting."

"And that's my fault," she cried incredulously. "Simply because I've been fortunate enough to have the things I want, I should what…turn it all over to some, some bum on the street! Devote my time to those less fortunate," she said in nasty singsong. She threw her hands up in the air.

"No. That's not it, and you know it. You'd be content with me working for your father or practicing a form of law that I hate in order to keep up the front of prestige and power and privilege. That's not who I am."

Her fine-boned features hardened, and hazel eyes glinted with fury. "That's what you think," she said with a tone of superiority in her voice. "You pretend to be holier than thou, but you're just like me. We were cut from the same cloth. You think that hiding behind a veil of the do-gooder makes you better." She laughed. "It doesn't, and it never will. Your name, where you came from, is who you are and who you'll always be. A Lawson!" She tossed her head.

Justin shook his head sadly. "That's exactly why we can never be together, Jasmine. Because I *am* more than a name and the weight that comes with it. What I intend to do with the weight that comes with the Lawson name is something you'll never be able to understand."

"Fine! Get out. Go save the world." Hot tears rolled down her cheeks. "You'll regret it. I swear to God, you will."

"No, I don't think so." He turned and walked out, shutting the door softly behind him and the sound of breaking glass hitting the door.

Chapter 6

Bailey had all but given up on seeing Justin again. With each day that passed, she put him further in the back of her mind. Her stomach didn't do that twirly thing every time the door to the Mercury Lounge opened—at least not as much as it once had, and she didn't imagine that she saw him in every other handsome face that she passed in the streets of Baton Rouge. She had all but moved on when Justin walked through the door.

Whatever lie she'd been telling herself—that she'd put all thoughts and budding feelings about him behind her—fell by the wayside when his searching eyes found her, and his smile lit a fire in her soul.

He moved through the crowd, and to Bailey it felt like slow motion. Her pulse began its rapid ascent while a tingling sensation rippled through her limbs as he came closer.

"Hey."

The pounding in her chest nearly drowned out his greeting. She swallowed and glanced away, focusing on the bar top. "Hi. What can I get you?"

"You could start by looking at me."

Her throat tightened. Her lashes rose, and her gaze connected with his. Big mistake. She sank into the depths of his dark eyes and was swept away.

He reached out his long, slender finger and touched her cheek. "That's better," he crooned. "I want to see those eyes."

Her cheek flamed beneath the tip of his finger.

"How have you been?"

"Fine." She took a step back. "And you?"

"Better now."

"Your regular?" she asked, trying to regain some clarity.

"Sure." She felt his eyes on her when she walked away. Bailey returned with his shot of bourbon.

"Thanks." He lifted his glass and took a sip without taking his eyes off her. "I was hoping that we could get together on your next night off."

Her heart thumped. "Get together?"

"Yes. Away from here. Just me and you."

She glanced away. "I don't think that would be a good idea."

"Why not?"

"I don't go out with my customers."

"Cardinal rule?"

"Something like that."

"Hmm." He tossed back the rest of his drink, pulled out his wallet and passed her his credit card.

"Is that all you're having?"

"Yep." He set his glass down and stared at her.

She drew in a breath, snatched up his card and walked to the register. Her hands shook as she processed the payment. Was that it? Was he simply going to walk out? She didn't give him much of a chance. *Fine. Go.*

Bailey returned with his receipt and his card. She placed them in front of him.

"Thanks." He tucked both away and slowly stood. "You take care."

"You, too," she managed to eek out.

Justin strode away, and Bailey's heart sank to the pit of her stomach.

For the rest of her shift she worked like an automaton. She handed out drinks, took orders and managed the bar all by rote. If anyone asked her what her night was like, she wouldn't have been able to tell them. The hours dragged by, and all she wanted to do was have her night end so that she could go home and crawl into bed. Thankfully, it was a weeknight, and they closed at eleven.

"You okay?" Mellie asked as they tallied up the night's receipts.

"Yeah. I'm fine. Why?"

"You seem a little out of it, that's all."

"I'm fine. A little tired."

"You go back to school in the fall, right?"

"Doesn't look good, but I'm still hopeful."

Mellie patted her on the back. "Everything will work out."

Bailey briefly glanced at her. "That's what I keep telling myself." She gathered her things and took the receipts and the cash drawer. "I'm going to put these in the safe, then I'm heading out. Get home safely."

"You, too. See you tomorrow."

Bailey went to the back offices to put the receipts and cash drawer in the safe and was surprised to see Vincent's light on. She tapped on his door.

"Come in."

"Hey, you're here late."

"Actually, I was waiting for your shift to end."

She frowned. "Oh. Is something wrong?"

He leaned back in his seat. "Come in for a minute. Close the door."

She did as he asked and sat in the chair in front of his desk.

"I've been thinking about things."

"Yes…" she responded with caution.

"You've been here for a while now, and I know how hard you work, and I tried to make sure that you were compensated for it, by promoting you to Assistant Manager."

Where was this going? Wherever it was, she didn't like the direction.

"And…I don't usually do this…but I want more."

"Excuse me?"

"I did all of that for you because I like you, Bailey. I like you a lot, and I was hoping that you could put aside whatever reservations you may have about relationships with your boss."

She blinked rapidly. "What…are you saying?"

"I'm saying that I want to take our business relationship and make it personal."

Her stomach did a three-sixty. "Vincent… I…"

He held up his hand. "You don't have to answer me now. Think about it. That's all I ask."

Bailey stood up slowly. This was the last thing she expected or needed. Her thoughts ran at a dizzying speed. There were no good choices. She needed her job and no matter what she did or said, things would never be the same. That much she was certain of.

"I, umm, I'll see you tomorrow."

He nodded. "Good night, Bailey, and please think about it."

Bailey walked out. Stunned could hardly describe how she felt. She closed the door behind her, made the deposit into the safe and mindlessly left the lounge. Her thoughts were still twisting in her head when she stepped outside, so much so that she thought for sure that she was imagining her name being called.

She glanced over her right shoulder, and there was Justin, perched on the hood of a gleaming Jaguar convertible as calm as if he was posing for a commercial. She squeezed her eyes shut and opened them, certain that she was seeing things. But she wasn't. Justin hopped down off the car and strode casually toward her, his hands slung in his pants pockets.

He stopped directly in front of her. "I hope I didn't scare

you." He held up his hand before she could respond. "And I'm not stalking you." He grinned that grin, and she knew she'd believe whatever he said.

"Okay," she said, dragging out the word. "What *are* you doing? You left hours ago."

"You made it pretty plain back there that you didn't mix business with pleasure, and I can appreciate that. And you don't go out with your customers." He gave a slight shrug of his left shoulder. "But I figured since I'll never be coming back to the Mercury Lounge again, you'd have to come up with some other reason why I can't take you to dinner."

Her throat went dry. She looked up and into his intense gaze, and there were a dozen comeback lines in her repertoire that she routinely doled out to would-be suitors at the job, but for the life of her, she couldn't think of any and didn't want to. She shifted her purse from her right shoulder to her left.

"Any reason you can think of?"

The air fluttered in her chest. "Not really."

Justin tossed his head back and laughed. "Woman, you sure give a man a hard way to go."

Bailey grinned. "So now what?"

He took her hand. "So now, you give me your number, and I'm going to call you, and you're going to tell me what night is good for you." He took out his cell phone. "Ready when you are."

Bailey dictated her phone number, and Justin added it into his contacts. "Done." He punched in her number and her phone trilled in her purse. She took it out. "Now you have mine." He put his phone back into his pocket. "Let me walk you to your car."

"It's on the corner."

They walked quietly side-by-side, and Bailey felt as if she was in a dream. She stopped in front of her Honda. She turned to him. "Thanks." She dug in her purse for her keys.

Justin took them from her shaky fingers, opened her

door and handed the keys back to her. He leaned down and placed a kiss so featherlight on her cheek that it sent a ripple through her limbs. Her heart banged in her chest. She ran her tongue across her bottom lip.

"Good night."

"Night." She slid in behind the wheel. He shut the door and stepped back.

Bailey managed to stick the key into the ignition and start the car. She slowly pulled off while stealing glances at him in her rearview mirror until she turned the corner, and he was gone.

Chapter 7

Bailey was grinning inside all the way home. She kept replaying their exchange in front of the Mercury Lounge and was still blown away that he'd actually waited outside, that he was willing never to come back simply because he wanted to honor her personal rule of not dating her customers. If it wasn't so late, she would call Addison.

By the time she shut her apartment door and kicked off her shoes, her cell phone rang.

"Hello?"

"Wanted to make sure that you got home safely."

Bailey's stomach flipped. "Yes. I just walked in the door."

"Good." He paused. "Rest well. I'll call you during the week."

"Okay. Good night." She pressed End on her phone then held the phone to her chest like a prize and did the happy dance. The heck with it being late. Waking Addison up from a well-deserved slumber with this hot bit of news was worth it.

After talking Addison's ear off for nearly a half hour, and listening to her squeals of delight and "I told you sos," Bailey bid Addison good-night, took a long, hot bath and then sank into her bed.

For the first time in quite a while, her night was filled with the sweet dream of possibility.

* * *

It had been only a couple of days since his talk with Jasmine, and already Justin detected the shift in the atmosphere at work. The partners were cordial and professional, of course, but there was an invisible distance between him and them that wasn't present before, as if they'd put up a shield to protect themselves from the inevitable fallout. Justin was sure that the only reason he hadn't been confronted by Mr. DuBois himself was because he'd been out of the country and was scheduled to return to the office that afternoon.

However, if he could withstand the rant of his father, who told him in no uncertain terms that he'd ruined his career and any chance at a partnership, and let that roll off his broad shoulders, he would deal with whatever Mr. DuBois had to say about "breaking the heart of his baby girl."

Justin turned his focus to the intellectual rights case that he'd been working on for the past few weeks. Although it was important to the client and he knew he would give it his best, this kind of work was so far removed from his real passion of working for those who really needed legal services but couldn't afford it.

His desk phone rang.

"Lawson."

"Mr. Lawson, Mr. DuBois is in his office, and he'd like to see you."

"Thanks, Rebecca. I'll be right there."

"Oh, and he said to bring the Warren file."

His sat up a bit straighter. The Warren file was the intellectual rights case that he was working on. This request didn't bode well.

"Sure. Thanks." He hung up the phone, put on his jacket and tucked the folder under his arm.

Mr. DuBois, Senior Managing Partner, had an office on the top floor. The elevator ride seemed to last an eternity, and when Justin strode down the long corridor, with the senior partners' offices on either side, to his boss's domain, it was the equivalent of walking the gauntlet. There were quick, sidelong glances from the secretaries and awkward smiles from the attorneys. Everyone seemed to know something was amiss.

Justin tapped on Mr. DuBois's door.

"Come in."

Justin walked in.

"Shut the door, Lawson," DuBois said, while covering the mouthpiece of the phone. He returned to his call.

Justin shut the door behind him and moved to the opposite side of the room. He took in the space. Massive and ostentatious were understatements. The room reeked of old money, power and prestige from the mahogany cabinets and bookshelves, to the persian rugs and twenty-seat conference table. The view from the floor-to-ceiling windows spanned one side of the room and overlooked the entire city of Baton Rouge. One wall was lined with degrees, certificates and photos of DuBois with his famous friends and wealthy clients.

"Have a seat, Lawson."

Here we go. Justin turned from scoping out the photos and approached DuBois's oversize smoked glass and cherrywood desk. He placed the Warren file on the desk. "The file you asked for." He unfastened his one-button jacket and sat opposite DuBois.

DuBois reached for the file and pushed it aside. He leaned back and rubbed his chin. "Are you happy here, Lawson?"

"Yes, sir, I am." It was a white lie but…what the hell. He rested his hands on the arms of the chair.

"You see yourself moving up within the firm?"

"I would hope so."

DuBois murmured in his throat. "To move up in the firm, I expect that my staff—all of them—are loyal, that they are dedicated to ensuring the success of the firm, first and foremost."

Justin waited for the ax to fall. He didn't have to wait long.

"There is little chance of success when the boss—me— is distracted by the actions of his employees."

"Sir?"

DuBois steepled his fingers. "I'm turning the Warren case over to Stevenson."

He tapped down his rising temper and leaned forward. "I've worked on that case for the past two months."

"I'm sure you've done the best you can with it." The dismissive tone was apparent.

Justin's eyes tightened at the corners. "You want to tell me the *real* reason why you're taking the case? Because I know it has nothing to do with my abilities in the office or in the courtroom, and if the client had an issue, I would have known about it."

DuBois glared. "The last time I checked, my name was on the door, and as long as it stays there, I don't have to tell you anything I don't think you need to know." He lifted his chin in challenge. "Maybe there's something you want to tell me."

Justin knew exactly what DuBois was doing, and he wasn't going to fall into a pissing match with him. He wanted Justin to get angry. He wanted Justin to steer the conversation in the direction of Jasmine. Justin wasn't going for it. He stood up slowly and refastened his jacket.

"If Stevenson needs any additional information on the Warren case, he can see me." He gave a short nod of his head, turned and walked out.

The faces were a blur as Justin moved steadily down the corridor toward the elevator. His jaw was so tight that his temples began to pound. He jammed his finger repeatedly on the down button as if that would magically make the elevator appear. Finally, it did.

It was clear that things were only going to get worse from here. DuBois was notorious for his ability to annihilate his opponents in the courtroom and in his life. Justin had now become his opponent, but he had no intention of allowing DuBois to pick him apart.

Justin returned to his office and shut the door. Once word got out that DuBois had pulled a case from him, it would only be a matter of time before everyone around him would know his career had derailed. He'd seen it happen to several other attorneys. Two eventually quit, one remained and basically did the required pro-bono work that big firms handled.

Justin leaned back in his seat and looked up at the ceiling. Everything happened for a reason. He'd been riding the fence long enough. He and Carl had been mapping out their future for months. There was no time like the present to seize the moment. How could he in good conscience stand up for others if he was unwilling to do the same for himself? He turned on his computer.

The confrontation with DuBois was the last bit of incentive that he needed. In one fell swoop he'd divested himself of the weight of a toxic relationship and a job that was sucking the life out of him.

He put his fingers on the keys and drafted his letter of resignation. He couldn't remember feeling better when he printed out the letter and signed his name. He smiled with satisfaction. This called for a toast.

Bailey was stepping out of a well-deserved shower after a long run in the park when her cell phone began to dance on the nightstand. Draped in her striped oversize towel that she loved, she quickly grabbed the phone and a jolt of excitement shot through her. "Justin."

"Hey, how are you?"

"Just getting out of the shower."

"I was hoping you were off tonight."

"As a matter of fact, I am. Why?"

"There's a jazz concert in the park tonight. Thought you might like to go if you don't have plans."

Bailey spun around in a giddy circle. "Hmm. What time?" she asked, not wanting to make it too easy.

"Show starts at nine. I thought I'd stop by the gourmet deli, get some sandwiches, snacks and some wine. We can throw down a blanket and eat outside."

She grinned as if he was asking her to accompany him to the inaugural ball. "Okay. Sounds good."

"Plus, I have some celebrating to do."

"Celebrating?"

"Tell you all about it tonight. What's your address? I'll swing by and get you by seven."

She gave him the information. "I'll be ready."

"See you soon." He disconnected the call.

Bailey floated around her bedroom getting ready and replaying the conversation over in her head. She never even asked who was playing tonight. Not that it mattered. It could have been the Three Stooges for all she cared. The main thing was that she was going to spend the evening with Justin and not as his bartender but his date.

She pulled out a pair of denim capri pants and a plain white spaghetti-strapped T-shirt. Accessories were the key with a simple outfit. So she selected a thick, bronze-toned metal bracelet, matching hanging earrings and a fabric belt that tied at the waist. She gathered up her springy spiral curls into a loose knot on the top of her head, added a splash of pink lip gloss and a hint of mascara. She appraised herself in the mirror. In all total her outfit might have cost eighty dollars, but she knew she looked like a million bucks. A plain canvas tote and simple platform slides finished off the look, and she was ready.

The doorbell rang and she went to the intercom. "Yes?"

"It's Justin. Ready?"

"Yep. Be right down."

"Oh, do you have a blanket?"

"Sure."

Bailey took one last look in the mirror, grabbed her tote, cell phone, keys and a blanket from the hall closet and headed out.

When she stepped outside, she wasn't sure what to expect or how she was going to feel seeing Justin, but no matter what she may have thought or felt, nothing prepared her for the impact of the real thing.

Justin was leaning casually against the side of an ink-black Jaguar that gleamed with a life of its own. He was surveying the neighborhood, which gave her a moment to take him in. He was just long, lean and fine. All caps. That's all there was to it. From the top of the sleek waves of his hair, the yummy caramel of his skin, the broad shoulders and hard chest with abs outlined in a black fitted T-shirt, down to the length of his powerful thighs and legs hidden beneath low-riding black jeans.

He turned, sensing her and slid the dark shades from his eyes. Her heart jumped. He came toward her and met her at the bottom step.

"Hey."

"Hey yourself."

He took the blanket from her, leaned down and kissed her cheek. "Good to see you," he said, soft as a prayer. He placed his palm at the small of her back and led her to the car, opened the door and helped her inside before rounding the car and getting in next to her.

Justin put his shades back on and turned the key in the ignition. "You look great," he said then put the car in Drive and pulled out.

Bailey adjusted herself in the seat and briefly wondered if he could hear her heart banging in her chest. *Damn, he smelled good.* "So…who's playing tonight?" she managed.

Justin shrugged slightly. "A local group. The name didn't ring a bell, though."

"You keep up with the local talent?"

"Pretty much. My brother, Rafe, plays. When he's in town he usually sits in on a couple of sets. So I try to keep up." He turned to her with a grin that made her stomach flip.

"Are you musically inclined, as well?"

"If you can count singing in the shower then I'm a star, baby."

Bailey laughed. "That remains to be seen."

He stole a quick glance at her before turning the corner. "I hope so."

Chapter 8

When they arrived at Greenwood Community Park, the crowds had already begun to file in. People were unloading coolers, lawn chairs, blankets and festive attitudes. There was a party energy in the air, and the buzz was that there was a special guest that would be making a surprise appearance.

"Wonder who it could be," Bailey said and took the blanket while Justin grabbed the cooler with their food.

"Looks like we're in for a show." He put his arm possessively around her waist and led them across the lawn to a space beneath a willow tree.

Bailey spread out the blanket while Justin took out some plates, napkins and clear plastic cups. "Hope you like shrimp po' boys." He took out the sandwiches and placed one on each plate. "There's chopped barbecue also."

"Oh, no, you didn't," she said, her stomach already screaming hallelujah.

Justin grinned. "I take that to mean that the menu meets with your approval."

Bailey sat with her legs tucked, spread a napkin on her lap and took the plate with the shrimp po' boy. "Catch me if you can," she teased and took a mouthwatering bite.

"I plan to do just that," he said in a slow, seductive tone that had nothing to do with eating sandwiches.

Bailey's pulse quickened when she glanced into his eyes and registered the intensity that danced there. For a moment she didn't breathe until he looked away and took out his choice of food.

"I got beer to go with the sandwiches." He plucked a bottle of Coors from the cooler. "The wine is for later." He winked.

Inwardly, Bailey smiled. This was a whole other side of Justin. She'd grown accustomed to seeing him order his bourbon and fancy dinners, show up in his expensive suits, not to mention the glitz and glamour that surrounded him the night of his grandfather's party. Justin Lawson was steeped in money, class and power. He was a man who could have anything and anyone he wanted. Yet, here he was, hanging out at a free concert in the park, eating sandwiches off paper plates and drinking beer from a bottle. Maybe there was a possibility for them.

Justin leaned on his elbow and faced her. "It's good to see you like this."

"Like what?"

"Relaxed. Unhurried. No distractions."

She briefly glanced away. "To tell you the truth, it's good to be out."

"What do you like to do in your free time?"

Bailey gave an abbreviated chortle. "Free time. Ha. What's that? With the hours that I put in at the Mercury Lounge, when I do have a day off, I usually sleep."

"We have to change that." He opened the bottle of beer and took a long swallow. "Hmm, forgot how good an icy-cold brew could be." He looked across at her. "How about we make a deal?"

"Depends. What kind of deal?"

"On your day off we plan to spend it together."

Her stomach fluttered. "How are you going to manage that? You have your day job."

The corners of his eyes tightened ever so slightly. "Let me worry about that."

She studied the calm but determined, unflinching look

on his face, the set of his mouth, and she knew that whatever Justin Lawson wanted he'd make a way to get it. "I think I'd like that."

"I just love it when negotiations go smoothly."

Bailey laughed. "Always the litigator."

"That's about to change."

She frowned. "Why? What do you mean?"

The voice of the emcee was amplified through the mic and filled the night air. "Good evening, and welcome to Greenwood Park's Jazz series. We have a show for you tonight. So sit back and enjoy the cool sounds of In Touch." The lights on the stage shifted to spotlight the quartet, and they launched into their first number.

"Tell you about it later," Justin said. He patted the space beside him. "Come. Next to me."

Bailey shifted her position and moved closer to Justin, close enough to feel the warmth of his body waft off him. She forced herself to focus on her surroundings and not the proximity of Justin, the feel of his hard thigh against hers, the woodsy scent of him that seeped into her pores and short-circuited her senses.

Fortunately, the band was excellent and able to distract her overly stimulated senses, and it wasn't long before they were both bobbing their heads and tapping their fingers in time to the music.

Now that the sun had fully set, the air had cooled, and a sensual breeze moved among the throng. Even in the midst of all the people, there was a feeling of intimacy that the music evoked that drew everyone closer—Justin and Bailey included. He'd adjusted his position so that his back was against the tree, and he'd pulled Bailey between the tight ropes of his thighs. He draped his arm loosely around her waist and intermittently he'd lean in and whisper something in her ear about the notes that were played, or a couple that he noticed or a star in the heavens that sparkled more than the others.

Each whisper against her neck, the words uttered like secrets, shimmied through her. Every now and then he would place his hand on her thigh, or tuck a stray wisp of hair behind her ear or trail the tip of his finger along her collarbone, and it took all that she had not to moan with every contact. There was a subtle sensuality, an understated eroticism about Justin that made it impossible to pretend that he was like every other man. He wasn't. The realization unmoored her because her thoughts got all crazy and fuzzy when she was around him, and her insides twirled, and her body screamed for him. All for a man that she barely knew. She'd always prided herself on her clearheadedness, and her focus, which was how she was able to put her own needs and wants aside, hold down two jobs and take care of her siblings for years. When she was around Justin, her sense of good and evil, left and right, up and down, were all screwed.

"How's the sandwich?"

Bailey blinked into reality. She angled her head over her shoulder. "Delish." She forced herself to take a bite. Her stomach was so jumpy with him being this close that she could barely swallow. Not to mention that food was the last thing on her mind. "How about you?"

"You want to know the truth?" He gently stroked her shoulder.

She didn't dare look at him. "Always."

He leaned down so that his lips brushed against her ear. "The only thing I've been able to think about is you—how you feel between my legs, that scent of yours that's driving me crazy, the texture of your hair, the softness of your skin. What it will feel like to make love to you."

Her breath hitched. She turned her head, and the hot sincerity that shot from his gaze lit the pilot light in her belly. She didn't move, didn't breathe, as he curved toward her, and his mouth slowly covered her own. He cradled her head in the palm of his hand and took full possession of her lips. A deep groan rumbled in Justin's throat while a sensation of light-headedness overtook Bailey. If he had not been holding her, she would have lifted away on the night wind. The music, the chatter, the world eased into the background, leaving only them imprinted in this one moment.

Justin slowly leaned back. The warmth of his chocolate eyes feasted on her face. He brushed his thumb across her slightly parted lips. Her eyes fluttered.

"Better than I imagined," he murmured.

Bailey swallowed. "Was it?"

The corner of his mouth curved into a smoldering grin. "Yeah, it was. So much better that I can't wait to taste you again."

Oh, damn. "You're very sure of yourself, Mr. Lawson."

"Yeah, I am. I'm sure that I've been walking in a fog since I met you. I'm sure that whatever it is that's pulling us together is something new for me, and I want to take my time figuring out what it is. And…I'm sure that you feel the same way."

Bailey slowly dragged her tongue across her bottom lip.

The air was suddenly filled with cheers and applause as the music came to an end, saving her from a response. The emcee took the mic. "Let's hear it for In Touch!" The applause rose again then slowly settled. "We promised everyone a special guest tonight, so please put your hands together for Tony award-winner Audra McDonald with her incomparable rendition of Billie Holiday."

The crowd went crazy.

"What!" Bailey squealed, and her eyes widened in stunned disbelief.

Justin tossed his head back and laughed, wrapped his arms around her waist, kissed her cheek, pulled her back against her chest and let the music and the voice do the rest.

"I still cannot believe we saw Audra McDonald," Bailey said, shaking her head while she fastened her seat belt.

"Pretty impressive for a first date, huh?"

Bailey cracked up. "I have to give it to you. I'm impressed, even if you had *no clue whatsoever* that she would be there."

"Ha! Minor detail."

"That's your defense, counselor?" She giggled and leaned back against the headrest.

Justin gave her a quick glance. His voice dipped and stroked her right where she needed it. "I'm far from resting my case." Justin winked, and her clit jumped. He turned his attention back to the road.

Bailey pressed her knees together and concentrated on breathing.

"Guess we have two things to celebrate."

"Two things?"

"A fabulous night *and* my personal celebration."

"Which you have yet to tell me about." She folded her arms.

"And we still have the bottle of unopened wine." He threw her a quick look.

"You're right. And where do you plan to open this *alleged* bottle of wine, counselor?"

Justin chuckled. "Alleged. Very funny." They stopped for a light. Justin angled his body in the seat to face her. "Well…there *are* some options. I can take you home, and you can invite me up, and I can tell you all about it, and then you can send me on my way. Or, I can take you to my place, I can tell you all about it, and I can fix you breakfast in the morning."

Heat scorched her cheeks.

Justin grinned and drove across the intersection. "Your choice. But the deal will be off the table when I hit the next exit. Right, my place. Left, yours."

"Are you serious?"

"Very."

The car seemed to slow.

"Exit coming up… Right or left?"

Her stomach flipped. "Right," she managed.

"Not a problem." He signaled, moved into the right lane and took the exit.

Chapter 9

Bailey's heart clapped in her chest. There was no doubt about Justin's intentions, and she'd just agreed to them. She linked her fingers together and stared out the passenger window. It's what she wanted—*needed* was a better word. She drew in a long, deep breath and stole a glance at Justin's profile. *Yes, needed.*

"You okay?"

Bailey's insides jerked. She turned. "Yes. Why?"

"You're sitting so close to the door, I'm thinking you might jump out."

The quip broke the knot of tension in her stomach, and Bailey laughed in relief. "Really?"

Justin chuckled. "Yeah, really." He made the turn onto the street that led to his house. The Lawson mansion loomed in front of them.

She had not been back to the house since the party. Without all of the people and food and decorations and music, it was much like any other home—only bigger. There was certainly a feeling of grandeur about the house, but there was still a sense of intimacy, from the simple but elegant decor to the array of family photos that told a story of not a dynasty but a real family.

Justin took Bailey's hand. "Make yourself comfortable." He led her into the living space. "I'll get the wine."

Bailey put her jacket and purse down on the club chair

while Justin took the bottle of wine and walked over to the minibar.

He popped the cork and poured two glasses. "Want to hear some music?"

"Sure."

"You pick."

Bailey strolled over to the stereo system that looked so complicated, a degree from NASA was needed to operate it. She skimmed through the revolving rack of CDs and selected some of her favorites—Kem, Luther Vandross and Kurt Whalum. "Here're my picks." She held them up in her hand. "But I have no idea how to work this thing."

Justin grinned. "Help is on the way." He crossed the room with the wineglasses and gave one to Bailey, tapped his glass against hers then leaned down and lightly kissed her lips. "Hmm, sweet." He turned his attention to the system, pressed a few buttons and the CD tables opened. He slid them in.

Bailey's insides vibrated every time he touched her. She couldn't even imagine what making love to him would feel like. Inadvertently she moaned.

Justin tipped his head toward her in question.

"The wine…it's really good." At least she was still thinking quick on her feet.

"Glad you like it."

Luther Vandross's sultry crooning wafted around them.

Justin took Bailey's glass from her hand and placed it on the side table. "Dance with me."

Bailey sputtered a nervous laugh. "Dance with you?"

"Yes." He stepped to her, slid one arm around her waist and eased her close. "Like this," he murmured against her hair.

Bailey's pulse roared in her ears. Her eyes drifted closed when she rested her head against his chest, and she silently prayed that he didn't feel her body trembling.

"This feels good." He held her closer while they swayed to the music.

Bailey lifted her head and dared to glance up. Justin was gazing right down at her, and the heat that flamed in his eyes started a campfire in her core. The world receded into the background as he lowered his head. She held her breath. Light as cotton his lips touched hers, and she melted into his body to deepen the kiss. The sweet tip of his tongue grazed her bottom lip, sending jolts of sizzling desire through her veins. Her soft moan of assent was all the invitation that he needed before fully capturing her mouth.

Justin's long fingers cupped the back of her head and threaded through the riot of tight spirals, then slowly trailed along the column of her neck while his tongue danced with hers. He pulled her tight against him, bending her back ever so slightly so that she could feel his growing need for her.

Bailey's sigh of desire was instantaneous, and she lifted her pelvis to meet the hard throb of his arousal. A groan seeped from his lips and into her mouth, erupting in her center.

The song ended, another one began, and they didn't miss a beat, finding their own rhythm that glided between the notes. Justin unsealed their kiss and braced Bailey's face in his hands. "I want you," he said, his voice thick with aching need. "I want to make love to you." His thumb stroked her cheek.

Her breath caught in her chest. It's what she'd longed for, this moment, this time. She'd seen them together, felt them together in her mind almost from the moment they met. *That* was pure fantasy. *This* was the real thing.

"Say yes."

She ran her tongue across her bottom lip, tasted him there. "Yes."

Without another word, Justin took her hand and led

her across the room, up the winding staircase and along the hallway to the suite of rooms at the end. He lowered the handle on the door and pushed it open. He turned in the threshold and looked at Bailey, searching for any sign of doubts, second thoughts. He backed into the expansive room. She followed and shut the door behind her.

Bailey quickly took in the room. Justin's essence filled it; from the decidedly sleek masculine furniture in deep chocolate woods and leather to the scent of him that teased her senses. French doors opened to a small terrace, and one wall held a mounted flat-screen television of undetermined size. The little things that personalized the space and made it feel lived in dotted the room: a pair of shoes by the side chair, a discarded jacket tossed across its back, a stack of magazines on an end table and his robe casually tossed across the foot of the king-size bed.

Justin came to her and placed his hands on her shoulders. "Change your mind?" he gently asked.

She shook her head, unsure of her voice.

He leaned down and kissed her so tenderly that it made her knees weak. His hands moved from her shoulders down her arms then snaked around her body. The kiss intensified, and their bodies connected.

Justin grasped the hem of her top and lifted it up and over her head. He clenched his jaw when he gazed upon the swell of her breasts. He placed a heated kiss on one side and then the other while he reached behind her and unfastened her bra. He slid the straps over her shoulders and plucked the delicate fabric away to fully reveal the tempting treasures that awaited him. He cupped the weight of her breasts in his palms and grazed the swollen nipples with his thumbs, bringing them to a tight head. Bailey's breath caught. Her chest rose.

He emitted a ragged groan as her fingers unfastened his belt and slid down his zipper.

Justin made quick work of relieving her of her pants and

panties before lifting her high in his arms to dip his face into the concave of her belly. She whimpered as the muscles of her stomach rippled beneath the erotic strokes of Justin's wet tongue. He walked with her in his arms across the carpeted floor to his bed and gently laid her down.

Bailey's heart pounded. Justin stood above her. The hard outline of his sleek body was outlined by the moonlight that slid through the open French doors. Her gaze was drawn from the broad expanse of his shoulders down to the rippling abs that led to the trail that gathered dark and thick around the heavy, long cock that lifted toward her. The dewy head glistened in the moonlight.

She had to touch him. Needed to touch him. Purposefully, she reached out. Her fingertips brushed the smooth skin. His hard member jumped in response. She wrapped her fingers around him and ran her thumb along the thick vein that throbbed on the underside of his sex. Power filled her when she heard his deep groan and felt the weight of his member pulse in her palm. She stroked him, slow and steady, letting only the tips of her fingers graze him. Each stroke stiffened him further. She could just make out the subtle tremors of his inner thighs. She ran her thumb across the dampened head, and he gripped her wrist.

"No more," he rasped. The dark embers of his eyes moved painstakingly slow across her face. Her fingers released him, and he kneeled on the side of the bed. "Turn over," he demanded.

Bailey's eyes widened. Her lips parted.

"Turn over."

She couldn't resist the command and did what he asked. Hot blood pumped through her veins. And then he was above her, his legs straddling her supine form. The tip of his erection brushed the curve of her spine. She gasped. Her body stiffened.

His tongue flicked that soft spot at the nape of her neck.

He clasped her arms that were at her sides and gently raised them toward her head and held them there.

Justin leaned forward and placed a kiss behind her left ear then her right. Her body shuddered. His tongue played with the tender skin, drifted along her collarbone and then slowly down the center of her spine. The nerves beneath her skin jumped and fluttered in response every time the wet heat of his tongue teased her. He blew his hot breath against her damp flesh, and the sensation was electric. Her soft whimpers aroused him as he continued down along her back to the dip then across the firm globes of her rear to the backs of her thighs. He teased her behind each knee and tenderly nibbled the strong calves. She shuddered and pressed her face into the downy fluff of the pillow.

"Don't hide. I want to hear you want me," he said. He spread her thighs and slid his arm beneath her, lifting her to press against the throb of his cock. Bailey flinched. He reached around her and stroked her slick split with his fingers.

"Ahhh…"

He teased the hard knot of her stiffened clit, and her entire body quaked. The sounds of her whimpers intensified and charged through his veins. He groaned, rose up and turned her onto her back.

Dark hunger sparked in his eyes. "Only if you want me," he said in a ragged whisper. "Tell me."

"Yes," she managed. She spread her legs and drew her knees upward.

Justin's jaw tightened as he held back the explosion that threatened to undo him. He rested back on his haunches, reached over to the nightstand and pulled out a condom packet. He tore it open and gave it to her.

Bailey's fingers shook as she slowly unrolled it over the length of him. He held his position above her and continued to finger her until her head thrashed against the pillow, and her hips rose and fell.

Justin braced his weight on his forearms and lowered his head to taste her mouth. The mixture of wine on her lips and tongue and her own sweet essence fueled him. His tongue danced with hers, savoring the flavor. She thrust her hips against him. He pulled back.

"Not yet." He captured one dark, full nipple between his lips and teased it with his teeth until she cried out in sweet agony then cupped her round rear in his palms and kneaded it until she trembled.

She was simpering with need, and that only intensified his want of her. He pressed the head of his sex against her slick opening. She gasped and gripped his shoulders. He pushed just a little to open her to him, and she cried out as her body gave way, and he pushed long and deep inside her wet walls.

Justin hissed through his teeth as the hot, wet warmth of her enveloped him.

The length and heft of him filled her in ways that she'd never before experienced. The fullness stole her breath and made her heart tumble in her chest. Shock waves jolted through her limbs as he began to move slowly in and out of her. By degrees her body adjusted to the feel of him, and she began to meet him stroke for stroke, lifting and rotating her hips, drawing groans that rose from his belly and tumbled from his lips. His body grew damp, as did hers as the pace escalated, and the sound of flesh slapping against flesh mixed with their moans and cries.

Justin rose up on his knees and pulled her hips tight against him as he plowed into her. Bailey gripped the sheets in her fists and bit down on her bottom lip, but it didn't stop her scream that vibrated through him.

The tremor started at the balls of Bailey's feet and scooted up her legs. Justin's buttocks tightened, and his sac filled and tightened. Bailey thrust her pelvis against him, and he blew like a volcano while her insides flexed and contracted in an orgasm that exploded in hundreds of white-hot lights.

"Oh, Goddddd…" Her neck arched. Her body vibrated as if hit with a bolt of lightning.

Justin's growl of release bordered on animalistic before he collapsed on top of her, breathing hard. He pushed her damp hair away from the sides of her face before cupping her cheeks and tenderly kissing her wet, swollen lips.

Bailey caressed his damp back, felt the hard tendons flex beneath her fingers. She had no words for the riot of feelings that poured through her. Thoughts and images of the two of them ran in a kaleidoscope through her head. Whatever she thought making love with Justin would be like, she was wrong. The empty space that lived inside her no longer echoed. The sound was dull and distant, receding into the background. She felt alive, vibrant, happy. Maybe it was only the effects of sexual release and afterglow. Whatever it was, she wanted to hold on to it for as long as she could.

She nuzzled Justin's neck, and she felt his smile. He lifted his head and gazed down at her.

"You okay?"

She nodded. "You?"

He chortled deep in his throat. "I passed *okay* a long time ago." He brushed his lips against hers, tasted the salty skin and sighed into her mouth. "Humph. Woman…you could easily become my guilty pleasure." He eased up off her and turned on his side. He braced his head on the palm of his hand. His eyes were at half-mast, only lifted by the satisfied smile on his lips.

Bailey ran her fingers down the length of his arm. Her eyes didn't leave his. "You never told me what you were celebrating." She took his hand, lifted it to her lips then drew the tip of his index finger into her mouth.

His breath hitched, and she sucked a bit harder. The dark pupils of his eyes grew larger.

"Tell me."

"What? That you're making me hard again sucking on my finger?"

"Oh, that." She tickled the tip of his index finger with her tongue. "What I asked you was to tell me what your surprise was," she said between little sucks.

He slowly extracted his finger from her mouth, turned onto his back and tucked his hands under his head.

"Well, I handed in my resignation today."

Her head snapped toward him. "What?"

"Yep." He glanced at her.

"But…why?"

He drew in a deep breath and exhaled. "It's been a long time coming. Today only sped up the process." He told her of the showdown with his boss as a result of his firmly telling Jasmine they had no future and how he'd come to his decision. "Things would only get worse at the firm if I'd stayed, and this way at least I can walk away with my head up and can move on to pushing my dream forward. Which is what I've wanted to do all along."

Bailey was a breath away from asking him if he could afford to leave his job when the reality of who he was kicked that thought to the curb. He was a Lawson. He could do what he wanted. Money was no object. The realization unsettled her. The fact that he could walk away from his job and pursue his dream was a stark reminder of just how different they were; how far apart their lives would remain.

"Something wrong?" Justin traced the outline of her ear.

She shook her head and forced a smile. "Nothing." She turned to face him and slid her leg between his. "It was wonderful," she whispered, easing close.

"It was more than wonderful." His eyes moved slowly over her face while he caressed the rise of her hip. "I want you to get used to having me in your life and many more amazing days and nights like this one."

Her heart thumped. She swallowed.

He leaned in and kissed her. His mouth moved over hers firm and insistent, sucking and teasing her bottom lip until her lips flowered, and his tongue dipped inside to savor her taste. And whatever notions she had in her head about their differences were pushed into the back of her mind as she welcomed him deep within her.

Chapter 10

Justin's eyes flickered open against the morning light that sifted through the draped windows. His body flexed and ached in a good way as memories of his night with Bailey rushed back. He turned his head. She was curled on her side, her wild hair shielding her face from him. Just looking at her got him hard. He stroked his shaft wanting to put it where it could find release—buried inside her.

Bailey stirred and sighed softly. She stretched her legs and arched her back. Justin was about to lose his mind watching her. He stroked a little faster. Bailey turned on her back and stretched her arms above her head, causing her full breasts to rise. The sheet slid down revealing her heavy mounds and the dark, hard nipples, and Justin's cock jumped in his hand. This was better than any strip show. Bailey moaned while she slid her hand down her body and between her legs. Justin nearly lost it. Sweat dampened his skin. He gritted his teeth as he watched the totally erotic show, imagining her fingers in all the slick places that his had been.

Bailey's lips parted. Her breathing escalated. "Ohhhh," she moaned. Her eyes fluttered open, and she turned to him. Her skin was flushed. "Justin," she said in a hoarse whisper. She reached for him, grabbed his hand and put it where hers had been. Her hips arched, and her eyes slammed shut.

Justin fingered her then put his slick fingers in his mouth to taste her. He pulled her on top of him. He cupped her breasts in his palms while she rose up on her knees and positioned herself before lowering her hips to suck him inside her.

"Good morning," she whispered before covering his mouth with hers and riding them both to satisfaction.

"Hope you like omelets," Justin said from his spot at the stove. He glanced over his shoulder and nearly dropped the spatula when he glanced at her barely covered in a towel and her hair dangling in wet tendrils around her face. "Hey."

"Hey yourself." She sauntered closer and stopped at the counter that separated them. Her gaze took in the broad bare back that curved into a perfect V, and the drawstring pajama pants that hung low on his narrow hips. She tugged on her bottom lip with her teeth.

"Coffee or juice?" He turned away to keep from doing something other than fixing breakfast.

"Coffee would be great."

"Help yourself." He ladled the omelet onto a platter and placed it on the center of the counter along with a bowl of fresh-cut fruit.

Bailey took the coffeepot off the heated inset on the table and poured coffee into a mug. "You want some?" She held up the pot.

The corner of his mouth rose. "That, young lady is a loaded question, especially with you standing in my kitchen with nothing on but a towel."

Bailey innocently glanced down at her scanty attire as if seeing it for the first time. "Oh...I can go change."

"Don't. I like the view."

Her cheeks heated. She lowered her gaze and slid onto a bar stool. "Now that you're unemployed, what are your plans?"

Justin sat opposite her and scooped fruit onto his plate and then a portion of the omelet. "Actually, I'll be going into the office for the next few weeks to clear up some pending cases and bring everyone up to speed on what I have on my desk."

Bailey nodded her head as she chewed on a forkful of omelet. "Mmm, is this feta cheese?"

"Yep. You like?"

"Very much. So...tell me more about your business venture."

His eyes lit up.

"It's been something I've been working on for about a year now. Along with my buddy Carl Hurley. He was with me the first night I came to the Mercury Lounge." He looked at her over the rim of his coffee mug. "I guess I need to thank him."

"For what?"

"He was the one that insisted I stay after he had to leave for a meeting. If I didn't, we may have never...gotten this far."

Bailey blushed. She took a mouthful of food.

"Anyway, it's called The Justice Project. Our goal is to handle cases for defendants that can't afford high-priced attorneys and those who we believe have been wrongly convicted."

"Really?"

He nodded. "That's the plan. We had scouted some locations for a small office. And there are more cases than we will probably be able to handle." He gave a slight shrug. "So this unscheduled departure is a blessing in disguise."

"Well...how do you go about selecting which cases to accept?"

"It's a process. Carl and I will review the case material, interview the defendant, any witnesses, and if we feel we can do some justice, we'll take the case." He angled his head in question. "Something's on your mind."

"No. I was just curious."

"I'm sure we'll need a staff," he said with a raise of his

eyebrow. "You already have some law school under your belt, and you plan to finish up, right?"

She focused on her plate and pushed her food around with her fork. "That's the plan."

"You don't sound very sure. I thought that's what you wanted."

"It is."

Justin studied her closed expression and decided to let it go. "So when do you go back to work?"

"Tonight. I should probably get myself together and go home."

"Now?"

"Yeah, I have a lot to do. Aren't you planning on going into the office?"

He heaved a sigh. "Around noon."

She nodded her head. "Looks like both of us need to get in gear." She pushed back from the table and stood.

Justin reached across the table and clasped her wrist. "What is it?"

"I don't know what you mean." She avoided looking at him.

"I feel like you did a one-eighty on me, and I'm not sure why."

"I don't know why you would think that."

He released her. "My bad." He took his plate to the sink. "Give me a few minutes to get dressed, and I'll drive you home."

"Thanks," she murmured and walked out of the kitchen.

Bailey put on her discarded clothing then stood in front of the bathroom mirror to try to put some order into her hair. She'd spent the most incredible night with a man she'd had a wet spot for since the night they'd met. Her body still hummed with pleasure. She smiled at the memories. There was no doubt that there was more than a physical connection between them. They vibed on so many levels. But… Her smile slowly faded. She didn't want to risk disturbing the magic, the one time in her life when there was someone for her—just her—by inserting the drama of her family life into the mix.

A sensation of guilt crept into her conscience. She couldn't turn her back on her siblings. She was the glue that held them together. The reality of her situation angered her. She shouldn't feel guilty for wanting her own life. But she did.

Roughly, she twisted her damp hair on top of her head and tucked it into an untidy knot. She turned away from her all-seeing reflection and returned to the bedroom to get her purse and shoes. Justin was pulling a shirt over his head. Her stomach twirled at the sight of him, the way his muscles rippled when he stretched and moved. She shook her head to scatter the hot thoughts that tried to dominate her good sense—which was telling her to go home.

Justin tugged down on his T-shirt, and Bailey came into his line of sight. "Ready?"

She leaned against the frame of the door. "Pretty much."

He nodded noncommittally, turned to his dresser and grabbed his wallet, keys and cell phone.

"Justin…"

He turned toward her with his brows raised in question. "Yeah… I… You were right."

"About what?"

"I did do a one-eighty."

"Wanna tell me why?"

She drew in a breath. "I want to…just not right now."

"My mama raised me to be a gentleman. I'd never make a lady do anything she didn't want to do." He gave her that half grin that sent shock waves up her spine. He strolled slowly toward her, tucked a finger under her chin and lifted it. "There's no rush…about anything. I don't plan on going anywhere."

Her heart knocked in her chest and for some reason,

her eyes filled with hot tears. She blinked rapidly, swallowed the knot in her throat and nodded her head. "Thank you," she whispered.

He pulled her into the protective arc of his arms and held her close. He didn't say a word. He simply held her, and to Bailey that was the most intimate thing he could have done.

Justin helped Bailey into her seat and shut the door, got in behind the wheel and flipped on the radio. The Tom Joyner morning show was on and host Cousin Tommy made a prank phone call that had them both laughing out loud. The prank call to a local pizza parlor was followed by the news that spewed out one bad story after the other, including the forecast that predicted a major storm complete with dangerous lightning and flash flooding.

They drove in companionable silence, bobbing their heads to the music and laughing at the outrageous members of the morning show. Before long, they were coming up on Bailey's street.

After they pulled onto her street and Justin got out to open Bailey's door, two police cars raced right down the block with their dome lights spinning. He held open the passenger door and helped Bailey out of her seat just as the nerve-jangling sound of police sirens wailed in the gray-tinged morning. Justin shut Bailey's door. His gaze followed the cars to the corner where they turned and then silenced, indicating that they'd reached their destination. He slowly rounded the car and fully took in the neighborhood. Several of the buildings on the opposite side of the street were boarded up while others were in disrepair. A small group of men of undetermined age sat on the steps of a corner house drinking out of brown paper bags. Justin walked Bailey to her front door. He didn't comment, but for the first time, Bailey saw her world through his eyes.

"Are you sure you have to work tonight? Weather report doesn't sound good."

"No choice. As long as Vincent opens the lounge... I'm on duty."

"I wish you didn't have to go in. These spring storms are notorious for always being worse than the forecast." He didn't want to tell her that what he was most concerned about was her coming home at night in this neighborhood. But it wasn't for him to say...at least not now.

"Thanks, but I'll be fine."

"Well, I'll try to stop by later this evening."

She forced a brave smile. "Okay. Look forward to it."

He leaned down and gently kissed her on the mouth. "You want me to come up?" he said against her lips.

"And neither one of us will get anything accomplished today." She pressed her finger to his lips.

"That would be the point, wouldn't it?" He gently nibbled the tip of her finger.

"Bye, Justin."

"Agggh, you wound me," he teased, pressing his hand to his chest and stumbling backward.

"Right." She shook her head and chuckled as she went up the three steps to her front door. "Talk to you later."

"Count on it." He waited for her to get through the front door before getting back into his car. He took one more look around before taking off.

Bailey opened the door to her apartment, and the sensation of being suffocated overwhelmed her. She shut the door, and at that moment saw just how small her place was. She'd grown used to the kitchen table that wobbled, the sink that dripped if you didn't turn the faucet just right and the sound of sirens that peppered the night. She tossed her purse on the used couch.

She'd prided herself on her "unique finds" as Addison put it, and made a habit of haunting the local flea markets

and used-furniture stores. She felt her one-bedroom apartment had an eclectic character. Now it seemed shabby. She
plopped down on the sofa and looked around. This is what
Justin would see. And she didn't want that. This was why
she didn't want to get involved with someone like Justin.
It was the road that her mother had taken, and it had ultimately taken her.

Oh, how easy it would be to slip into a lifestyle that she
knew Justin could offer. All of her worries would be over.
She drew in a long, slow breath. She wasn't her mother.

Her cell phone buzzed inside her purse. She dug around
and pulled it out. Her sister Apryl's number lit the face
of the screen.

"Hi, sis," Bailey greeted. At least Apryl rarely needed
money. But if men were dollar bills, her baby sister would
be a wealthy woman. "What has you calling so early?"

"I *do* have a job that requires me to be at my desk
by nine," she playfully tossed back. Apryl, at the tender
age of twenty, worked for an up-and-coming urban men's
fashion magazine as a copy editor. A job that suited her
perfectly. Apryl had always done well in school, and the
chance to meet gorgeous men on a regular basis was right
up her alley.

Bailey chuckled. "Okay, so what's up?"

"Well…" she lowered her voice. "There is this *f-i-n-e*
brother who has been doing a shoot here all week, and
well…we kind of hit it off. I was wondering if you could
hook me up a nice table at Mercury."

Bailey's brows pinched together. "Why are you taking him out?"

"B…get with the program. Hello…women take men
out all the time."

"They do?"

Apryl sighed into the phone. "Can you do it or not?"

"I guess so. When?"

"Tonight."

"You heard about the storm, right?"

"Oh, yeah," she said, dragging out the last word. "Are you working tonight?"

"Yes."

"Okay, well, if it looks too dicey we can make it another night."

"Fine, sis. Let me know when you know."

"Will do."

"Great," she said, cheerfully. "Anyway, gotta run. Hugs."

"Hugs." Bailey dropped her phone back into her purse and pushed up from the couch. She had some errands to run, and nothing would get done sitting on the couch.

She went into her bedroom and looked at her queen-size bed that resembled a doll bed compared to Justin's. It would never work. They were from two different worlds. But for once she was going to be selfish and do this for her...at least for a little while.

Chapter 11

Justin arrived at the office a bit before noon. The moment he pushed through the glass doors to the reception area, he could feel the change in the air. Dina, the front desk receptionist, was almost apologetic in her greeting and wouldn't look him in the eye. The associates that he passed in the hallway murmured veiled greetings. He stopped at his assistant's desk to check for messages.

"Mr. Dubois was looking for you. He wanted to see you when you got in."

"Thanks. Tell him I'll be there in a few minutes."

She picked up the phone while Justin walked into his office and shut the door.

He was sure that Dubois would have been more than happy to accept his resignation, considering the conversation they'd had. So he couldn't imagine what else they had to talk about. He made a couple of calls then took the elevator ride to Dubois's office.

"He's waiting for you," Dubois's secretary said. "Go right in."

"Thanks." He adjusted the knot in his silk tie and strode toward the closed door. He knocked lightly and went in.

"You wanted to see me."

"Lawson. Have a seat." He pursed his lips and leaned back in his chair.

Justin took a seat opposite Dubois's desk.

Dubois reached for the letter on the desk. Justin knew what it was. He waved the letter in front of him then tossed it on the pristine desk. "This is the route you decided to take." It was more of a challenge than a question.

"The right one. It's clear that we've come to a crossroads. I'll clear up my cases, bring my replacement up-to-date and be out of here by the end of the month." He stared him in the eye until Dubois looked away.

Dubois stood, a tactic that Justin knew was only to create a sense of control. "Don't be a fool. You have a future here."

"Do I?"

His eyes tightened at the corners. "My employees don't walk out on me. *I* let them go."

Justin didn't respond.

Dubois blew out a breath filled with frustration. He looked hard at Justin, who didn't flinch as most would have done. "Whatever issues you may have with my daughter shouldn't interfere with your job here."

He'd finally put it out on the table. Justin crossed his right ankle over his left knee. "It never did."

Dubois's jaw tensed.

This wasn't a matter of Dubois wanting him to stay. He simply was not used to anyone defying him. Justin knew this, and that's why he had the upper hand. If he'd decided to stay, he could probably negotiate for whatever he wanted. However, it was too late for that. He'd made up his mind. Dubois would have to find a way to deal with his wounded ego.

Dubois slid his hands into his pockets. "As I said, Lawson, I think you are making a big mistake. Most would have been begging to stay. Not you." He snorted. "But…I respect you for it." He lifted his chin.

Justin's brows rose in surprise. "Thank you, sir." He knew that wasn't easy for Dubois to say.

"Keep me posted on the progress of your cases."

Justin stood. "I will."

Dubois turned away, ending the meeting.

"Thank you for the opportunity."

Dubois murmured a grudging acknowledgment deep in his throat. Justin smiled to himself and walked out.

When he returned to his office, Carl was waiting for him.

"You could have given me a heads-up, man."

Justin held up his hand. "I know. It wasn't planned."

Carl plopped down in a chair. Justin closed the door.

"So…what happened?"

Justin ran down to Carl what had transpired between him and Dubois and what prompted him to file his resignation, up to and including the last conversation.

Carl lowered his head and shook it slowly. "Wow. So now what?"

"So now I can move ahead with the plan—full-time."

Carl massaged his right knee. "I'll do what I can from here. I can't say I'm ready to follow in your footsteps."

"I don't expect you to. You have a wife to think about. I'll work on getting us set up. You jump in when you can."

"Cool."

"Knee acting up again?"

"Yeah. Played a short game of pickup last night." He chuckled. "Not as young as I used to be."

Carl could have made it to the NBA, but he was injured in his sophomore year of college, and his knee had never been the same.

"Where were you last night? I called you. Wanted to see if you wanted to play."

Justin grinned. "I was with Bailey."

Carl's eyes widened. "Get out. So…what happened?"

"I don't kiss and tell. But I will say it was…great."

"Ha! My man."

"I really dig her, man."

"I hear a *but* in there."

Justin leveled his gaze with Carl's. He knew him all too

well. "I took her home this morning and—" he hesitated "—she lives over on Chestnut."

"Hmm. Rough area."

"I know. I don't like the idea of her having to come in and out at all kinds of crazy hours from her job."

"Not much you can do about it unless you're going to morph into her sugar daddy and set her up somewhere."

The idea ran pleasantly through his head. "I wouldn't mind waking up to Bailey every morning."

"Say what?" Carl croaked. "She got you whipped like that already?"

Justin grumbled in his throat. "I like her. A lot. End of story."

"Told you, man. The right woman can change your whole mind."

"Don't you have work to do?"

Carl gingerly pushed up from his seat. "Don't hate the messenger." He chuckled. "Talk to you later."

"Yeah. Later."

Justin sat down behind his desk and thought about his comment to Carl. He'd never considered living with a woman or taking care of one. Bailey was different. She wasn't like the women he'd known. She clearly didn't have everything handed to her. She worked hard for whatever she wanted. She was smart, sexy as all hell and easy to be with. When he made love to her…it was like coming alive. Yeah, he liked her. A lot.

Chapter 12

Vincent came behind the bar. "You going to be okay getting home?"

"I'll be fine." Bailey wiped down the bar top and continued stacking glasses in the rack for washing.

"I can drive you home. You'd be a lot safer in my truck than your car in this weather."

Her honey-toned eyes flicked toward him. Their once, easygoing friendship had grown tense since he'd made his overture several weeks earlier. She'd made it a point to keep her distance and steer clear of having to respond to his "offer." This was the first time they'd actually been in the same space long enough to have a conversation. She moved farther away.

"We haven't had a chance to talk in a while." He lined up the bottles on the shelf, something he never did. "I wanted to give you some time and distance…to think about what I said."

Her heart pounded. "Vincent." She turned to face him and folded her arms. "We have a good working relationship, and I truly appreciate everything that you've done for me." She paused. "I'm seeing someone and even if I wasn't, I don't think that taking a business relationship and making it personal is wise, or something that I would do. I hope you understand that."

His gray eyes grew stormy, darkening like the skies. "I see."

"I don't want this to affect anything."

He placed another bottle on the shelf. "Get home safely." He turned and walked away.

Bailey let out a breath she'd held and realized that she was trembling inside. The look in his eyes actually chilled her. She made quick work of closing out the register and took the night's receipts to the safe. There was no way she was going to try to make it to the bank. She'd take care of it in the morning.

On her way out, she checked her phone. Apryl was supposed to have stopped by. She was sure the weather was a deterrent, but she was surprised that she hadn't heard from her sister. Knowing Apryl, she was more than likely curled up with her new man somewhere. Something she wished she was doing instead of navigating the flooded streets of downtown Baton Rouge.

The windshield wipers were working overtime, but she managed to see enough to pull over so that she could make the call to Justin. She put on her hazard lights, just in case, and pulled her cell phone from her purse. Just as she was ready to call, the phone rang in her hand. She didn't recognize the number. She pressed the talk icon.

"Hello?"

"Is this Bailey Sinclair?"

"Yes. Who is this?"

"I'm calling from the admitting office at St. Barnabas Hospital. Your sister Apryl was in a car accident. She asked that you be called."

"Oh, my God. Is she all right?"

"She's listed as stable. Do you think you can make it to the hospital?"

Bailey peered into the night, looked around to try to get her bearings. "Yes, yes. Um, I'll be there as soon as I can."

She tucked the phone into her purse, gripped the steering wheel and lowered her head. She whispered a prayer.

The drive to the hospital was nerve-racking to say the least. So many of the streets were flooded that she had to detour around them, and lights were off in some areas making it nearly impossible to see in front of her. Shaken, she finally arrived at the emergency entrance of the hospital, found a parking spot and raced inside.

"My sister Apryl Sinclair was brought in. She was in a car accident," she blurted out the instant she reached the intake desk.

The clerk behind the counter checked her computer screen. "Do you have ID?"

Bailey rolled her eyes in annoyance and fished in her purse for her ID, practically shoving it in the woman's face.

The woman looked it over and handed it back. "Sorry, but we have to be careful," she said, mildly soothing Bailey's ire. "Your sister was admitted, but they haven't taken her to her room yet. She's still in the emergency area. Walk straight through those swinging doors. You'll see a reception desk. Someone there can tell you where she is."

"Thank you."

"Good luck." She smiled.

For an instant Bailey felt bad about the awful things she was thinking about doing to the woman. "Thanks."

She hurried down the corridor and through the swinging doors. The nurses' station was on her right. "Hi. My sister Apryl Sinclair was brought in earlier. Car accident." Her heart was racing so fast she could barely catch her breath.

The nurse checked her register. "Yes. She's in the fourth cubicle down on your left. The doctor is with her now, I believe."

"Thank you." She raced off. Curtain number one, two, three, four. She stopped, steeled herself, and said a silent prayer for strength, not knowing what to expect when she pulled the curtain back. She didn't have to. A young, ready-for-television-looking doctor pulled the curtain back and stepped out, nearly colliding with Bailey.

"Sorry," he said, grinning, showing deep dimples in his smooth chocolate face. "I'm Dr. Phillips. Relative?"

"Yes, Doctor. I'm her sister." She tried to peek over his height and broad shoulders to get a glimpse at the body beneath the white sheet. "How is she?"

"Very lucky. She has a concussion, bruised ribs and a badly sprained wrist. The car didn't fair as well, I understand."

Bailey pressed her hand to her mouth and sighed in relief. "Can I see her?"

"Sure, but only for a few minutes. They need to get her to a room."

"How long is she going to have to stay?"

"At least overnight. The main thing is the concussion. We want to monitor her for the next ten to twelve hours. If everything looks good tomorrow, say midday, she can go home. She'll experience headaches for a while, and she'll need some help until her ribs and wrist heal, but other than that, she should be fine." He flashed those dimples again. *Perfect for Addy.* "Thank you, Dr. Phillips."

"She may seem a little out of it. But it's to be expected. I don't want you to be alarmed."

Bailey nodded. She tugged in a breath and stepped behind the curtain. Her heart jumped at seeing her sister appear so helpless. Her eyes were closed, and there was an IV in her arm. Her left hand was in a soft cast. Bailey slowly approached. She stroked her sister's fingers.

Apryl's eyes fluttered open. "Sis," she croaked.

"Hey," she said softly. "How are you feeling?"

Apryl groaned. "Like I was in a car accident," she said, trying to make light of her situation.

There was a bruise on her cheek, and her eyes looked

slightly swollen. Her lip was cut, but other than that, she looked like herself. That was a relief.

"The doctor said that you'll probably go home tomorrow. You're going to stay with me until you're feeling better. No argument."

She tried to smile but winced instead.

"What happened?" Bailey pulled up a chair and sat next to the bed.

"It was so freaking dark, and the rain was crazy," she said in a halting voice. "The next thing I knew I'd hit a divider."

"Where in the world were you going in this weather?"

"I was going to see John, the guy I was telling you about. Never made it."

Bailey slowly shook her head. "The main thing is you're okay." She lightly squeezed her hand.

"You mean you're not going to fuss me out?"

"Not this time." She offered a soft smile. "I'm just happy that it wasn't worse."

A nurse pulled the curtain back. "We're ready to take you to your room, Ms. Sinclair." An orderly followed the nurse into the tight space.

Bailey squeezed by and stepped out while they unlocked the wheels on the bed and connected the IV to a hook on the bed.

"What room will she be in?" Bailey asked as they began to wheel Apryl out.

"Third floor. Room C14."

"Thank you."

"You won't be able to come up, but you can come back in the morning." She offered an apologetic smile.

"Okay." Bailey walked with them to the elevator and held Apryl's hand the entire way. "I'll see you in the morning." She tenderly brushed her forehead then placed a kiss there. "Get some rest."

The elevator doors opened, and they pushed the bed in-

side. Bailey finger-waved at her sister as the doors closed.
For several moments she stood there staring at the door
and replaying the events of the evening. Suddenly, a wave
of exhaustion overtook her, and she felt like her body was
going to give out. She squeezed her eyes shut for a moment
and took deep breaths. She opened her eyes and looked
around at the rush of nurses and doctors, the anxious faces
of family members, heard the clang of metal, orders being
barked out and the cries and moans of the sick and injured.
She had to get some air.

When she stepped outside, the wind seemed to have
died down, but the rain continued. All she wanted to do
was go home and crawl into bed. She dashed for her car and
stepped into a puddle that reached her ankles. Perfect. By the time she got to her car she was soaked through
and through. Her shoes were soggy, and her clothes were
sticking to her.

"Just get me home," she said and turned on the ignition.

The drive home was riddled with obstacles from stalled
cars to flooded streets. Finally, there was daylight at the
end of this seemingly endless tunnel. She was two blocks
away from home, and then her car shut off in the middle
of the street.

"Oh, hell, no. Not tonight." She turned the car off then
back on. All she heard was a click. She tried again. And
again. *Click. Click.* She pounded the steering wheel in fury.

Clearly she couldn't stay there. She gathered her belongings, checked the glove compartment and took out
all of her important papers and stuck them in her purse.
She checked around the interior of the car for anything of
importance then got out. She locked the door and prayed
that it would be there in the morning.

The streets were beyond dark. There were no street-
lights and only intermittent light coming from scattered
windows. By the time she reached her front door, she was

beyond soaked and felt like a leaking pipe with water dripping off her from everywhere. She left a watery trail up the darkened staircase.

She opened her apartment door, whispered a silent prayer and flicked on the light switch. Nothing. She felt her way into the kitchen and found two old candles in the overhead cabinet. She was sure she had a flashlight somewhere but didn't have the energy to look for it. She lit a candle and lighted her way to the bathroom, where she peeled out of her clothes and left them in a wet heap on the floor. She didn't have the energy for the shower that she desperately needed, but instead dried off with a towel, took her nightshirt off the hook on the back of the bathroom door and put it on. She padded back into the kitchen and poured herself a glass of water before plopping down on the couch. She blew out the candle, and the room was suffced in darkness. Better to hide the tears of exhaustion and frustration.

The sound of sirens and the oppressive heat woke Bailey the following morning. She blinked against the blazing light coming in through the window and slowly sat up. Every muscle in her body ached from having fallen asleep on the couch. She rotated her neck and then pushed up from the couch. Her knees ached. The clock on the microwave was flashing. At least the electricity was back on. She walked to the window and looked outside. The neighborhood was slowly coming to life, and then the events of the night before stiffened her spine. Her sister!

She hurried over to her purse and pulled out her cell phone. She plugged it in and while it charged she took her much-needed and long-overdue shower. When she'd finished, she felt human again. She checked her phone and there were three messages from Justin. Her stomach fluttered. She went into her voice mail and listened to his calls. He sounded genuinely worried and asked her to please call him no matter what time. His last call was at 3:00 a.m. She tugged on her bottom lip with her teeth, literally biting back a smile. He was thinking about her. He was worried about her. She would call him back and let him know she was fine.

But, first things first. She needed to call the hospital and get the update on her sister, which she did. The on-duty nurse told her that the doctors had not made their rounds and would make a determination then about her discharge. Rounds would be completed about 11:30 a.m. She could call back after that time. Bailey thanked the nurse and hung up. According to the clock on her phone it was just after eight. She had some time to get her place in order for her sister and fix some coffee to get rid of the remaining cobwebs.

With a mug of coffee in hand, she checked her phone that was now fully charged. She sat down at the kitchen table and called Justin. He picked up on the first ring as if he'd been watching the phone, waiting for her call.

"Bailey! I was worried sick. Are you all right?"

"A little worse for wear but I'm okay. Sorry I missed your calls. My phone was dead. We didn't have any power…and my car… Oh, damn."

"What? What happened to your car? Were you in an accident?"

"Not me, my sister Apryl." She ran down the events of the evening up to her car dying on the street.

"I'm getting dressed right now. You stay put."

"I can take care of it."

"I know you can. That's not the point. Wait there."

"Justin, you don't have to come. I can handle it."

"Goodbye, Bailey. I'll be there soon."

"Justin!"

"Goodbye, Bailey." The line went dead.

She sucked her teeth in an attempt at being annoyed, but she was bubbling inside. As much as she may protest, she didn't want to deal with the day ahead alone. Now she didn't have to.

Chapter 13

"Girl, you had some kind of night," Addison said. "Is your car still there?"

"I sure hope so." She sighed.

"At least Justin is coming. He'll take care of everything. And worst case, he can take you to pick up Apryl from the hospital."

"You know that depending on men rubs against me like sandpaper. Dependency leads to nothing but trouble and heartache."

"Don't even start with that mess. Independence is fine. Shouting *I am woman, hear me roar* from the rooftops is fine, but there comes a time when there's nothing wrong with asking for and accepting help from a man. It's not going to diminish your womanhood. Did it occur to you that he's doing this because he cares?"

"Too late to stop him now," she groused. "But let me tell you about this gorgeous doctor that is taking care of Apryl. Perfect for you."

"You are always so concerned about and fixing everybody else's life."

"Don't go there again, Addy. Not today." She had to fix and worry about everyone else. It was the only way she could keep the past at bay, but it was always lurking in the shadows, following her wherever she went. What scared her in a place deep in her soul was that she was mirroring the life of her mother—as much as she tried to fight it.

Phyllis Sinclair was forty-seven when she took her own

life. Saddled with three kids and no man. That was what drove her mother to do the things that she did and to ultimately take her life. Her mother had been gone for five years, and she missed her every single day. The only way she could avoid the path that her mother had taken was never to need or depend on a man. She would maintain her independence at any cost.

"I have to go, Addy."

"Okay, one last thing."

"I couldn't stop you if I wanted to."

"Fine." She paused a beat. "Let him help you, B…this one thing. Accept it gracefully. If for no other reason than because it will feel good, girl." She laughed.

Bailey pushed out a breath. "Okay, you've badgered me into submission."

"That's what besties are for. Hugs."

"Hugs back." Bailey put down the phone, looked around her apartment and made a mad dash to put everything in order. Justin had never been to her apartment. Suddenly, the sheer white curtains that let in all the sunshine on Crescent Street looked cheap and flimsy. The crack above the sink seemed to be grinning at her. The bedroom was not much better. Her bed, that was always her oasis, appeared bland and insignificant. She closed her bedroom door just as the bell rang. She'd meet him downstairs. There was no reason for him to come up.

Bailey opened the downstairs front door, and that indescribable sensation sizzled through her at the sight of him. The only reason to be as damned fine as Justin Lawson was to torment all the women who couldn't have him.

"Hey," she said, playing it casual as she trotted down the three steps.

"Hey yourself." He looped his arm around her waist and pulled her close. Her chin brushed against the baby-soft fabric of his gray fitted sweater. The tempting V at the neck dared her to touch him. He took her mouth and her breath away as if they were his to own.

"I needed that," he murmured against her mouth.

Bailey was on fire. Her body of its own will yielded to him, longing for him to command it to do whatever he wanted.

"Do you smell this good all over?" He breathed into her ear before easing back.

His eyes were endlessly dark as they descended upon her, making her heart race and her pulse roar in her ears to block out the world around them. It was only the two of them until the blare of several car horns intent on out-blasting each other snapped the spell in half.

"Woman, you could make me forget what I need to do." He grinned that sly, sexy grin, and the dampness between her legs intensified.

"So, where's the car?"

Bailey blinked. "Um, two blocks over." She pointed in the direction.

"Did you call a tow service yet?"

"No. My phone was dead last night…and this morning…I want to make sure it's still there." She didn't know what she was going to do if it needed to be towed.

"It will be, and if it's not, I'll take care of it." He took her hand.

His long, slim fingers enveloped her hand. She wanted to tug away, remind him that *she* would take care of it. Somehow. She drew in a breath, and even Addison's warning words didn't stop her from verbalizing the fear that lurked in her heart. "You really didn't have to do this." She felt his entire body tighten.

Justin stopped walking. "What exactly shouldn't I have done—come to see if I can offer some assistance to a woman that has taken up residence in my head, be here if she wants to talk or just be a decent kind of guy who doesn't want to see a hardworking, beautiful, fiercely independent, sexy-as-hell woman stranded? Any of those strike a chord?"

Bailey twisted her lips to keep from grinning. "Fine. The defense rests."

"Hey." He lowered his head and lifted her chin with the tip of his finger. He looked deep into her eyes. "Never think or imagine in a million years that you'll ever have to be on the defensive with me. Okay?"

She nodded her head. "Okay."

He took her hand again, and they continued on for the block and a half and there was her car, right where she left it.

Bailey pressed her hand to her chest and exhaled in relief. "Thank goodness it's still here."

Justin squeezed her hand and kissed the top of her head. They hurried over to the car, and a quick inspection turned up no apparent damage, not even a parking ticket.

"So far, so good," Bailey said before unlocking the driver-side door. She got in behind the wheel and turned the key in the ignition. Nothing happened.

"I'll call a tow service," Justin offered as he slid into the car next to her. He pulled out his phone, scrolled through his contacts, found the number and placed the call. Shortly after, he was giving his info and then asked Bailey for her plate number. "They said about a half hour."

"Thank you." She released a breath of relief.

"What time do you need to be at work?"

Bailey groaned and pressed her hand to her forehead. "Late shift. Seven to twelve. I'm going to need to get a rental."

"You can use my car."

She snapped her head toward him. "Your car?" Her brows knitted.

"I can drive...my other car."

Her cheeks heated. Of course he would have more than one car. "I couldn't ask you to do that. I can get a rental."

Justin lowered his chin. "Let me ask you something. Why is it so hard for you to accept any help…at least from me?"

The slight hitch in his voice caught Bailey by surprise. She tightened her grip on the steering wheel. "It's not you," she whispered.

"Okay. That's a good start. Then what is it? Seriously."

"It's complicated."

"I'm listening."

She couldn't look at him. "It's… I've seen firsthand what depending on someone can do to you."

Justin rocked his jaw. "Seen? Who? What did you see that was so damned foul that it keeps you second-guessing and keeping at arm's length anyone that wants to get near you?"

Bailey's features flinched. Her throat worked as the words clung there, stuck against her tongue and struggled to get past her pinched lips.

"My mother," she finally blurted.

Justin kept his surprise behind a neutral expression. "Must have been rough."

Bailey reached for the handle and opened the door. "It was." She needed air. "And I really don't want to talk about it." She stepped out of the car.

Through the car window, Justin watched Bailey pace. He didn't know what she meant by "her mother" but whatever happened, it had dug a deep hole in her soul that had been refilled with doubt, suspicion and fear. He'd leave it alone for now, but he had every intention of digging all of that crap out and filling her up with what she really needed.

He took out his cell phone and spent the waiting time answering a couple of emails and checking into the office to let his assistant know that he would be there by early afternoon. He spotted the tow truck coming down the street, got out of the car and went around to stand next to Bailey. He draped his arm around her shoulder and felt her relax against him.

The driver checked the car, hooked it up to his truck and gave Justin instructions to the garage where it would be taken.

Bailey thanked him as she watched her precious baby being towed away.

"So what do you want to do, get a rental or drive my car?"

Bailey slid her gaze across Justin's polished two-seat Mercedes Benz. "Um, maybe I should get a rental. I wouldn't forgive myself if something happened to your car."

Justin chuckled. "It's only a car, Bailey. But if you feel more comfortable, do the rental. The family has an account with a private car rental agency. I'm sure I can get you something you'd feel more comfortable with."

The gleam of sunlight bounced off the hood of the car. "Well…maybe the Benz won't be so bad."

Justin tossed his head back and laughed. "That's what I'm talking about! Come on, get behind the wheel and get comfortable. We'll go pick up your sister, and I'll take a car service from there."

Bailey got behind the wheel and sighed as the lush leather seats cushioned her like a lover. The brand-new, off-the-showroom-floor scent still lingered. The dashboard was a series of blue lights and glass and panels. Daunting. She turned the key in the ignition, and the engine purred to life. She gave Justin a quick look, and he simply adjusted his seat back and closed his eyes. She drew in a breath and pulled off.

At the first stoplight, Bailey scanned the dash to figure out what button to press to turn on the radio. She finally found the icon, and the local jazz station joined them for the ride. Containing a satisfied smile, Bailey maneuvered the dream machine in and out of the growing traffic, or rather the Benz did the driving. The ride was so smooth and the vehicle handled so well, it was akin to gliding on a cloud. It would be so easy to get used to this.

She stole a quick glance at Justin, who was completely in relax mode, eyes closed, head back, fingers lightly tapping the armrest in time to the music. Not a care in the world. The life of money and privilege.

Not too long after, the hospital loomed ahead. Bailey drove into the visitors' parking lot. Justin opened his eyes and sat up.

"Hmm. Safe and sound." He yawned. "Ready?"

It was on the tip of her tongue to tell him that he didn't have to come with her, but this time she refrained from what, to her, was instinctual. "Sure." She swallowed. "Thanks."

"I was supposed to call and find out what time they were releasing her," Bailey was saying as they pushed through the revolving glass doors. "I totally forgot."

Justin checked his watch. "If the hospital is true to form, she won't be released before noon."

They stopped at the information desk and received passes to enter the ward.

"Why is that?" She pressed the button for the elevator.

"After twelve they can charge for another day." He gave an offhand shrug. "Capitalism."

The elevator doors opened. Justin and Bailey stepped aside to let the passengers off, one of whom was Dr. Phillips.

"Bailey." He smiled warmly.

"Dr. Phillips. I was coming to pick up my sister. How is she?"

The elevator doors closed.

"She had a restful night. The tests look good, so I've already put in the discharge order along with instructions for aftercare."

"Thank you." She extended her hand, which he shook.

"Thank you so much. Dr. Phillips, this is Justin Lawson."
She turned her attention to Justin.

The two men shook hands. "Lawson...Senator Lawson's son?"

"That would be me," he said without humor.

"Pleasure to meet you. Tell your father he has my vote in the next election."

Justin only returned a shadow of a smile.

"Well, make sure your sister gets plenty of rest. No driving while she's on the medication. It's pretty strong. She should come back in two weeks for a follow-up, but of course if there are any problems, she should come in right away."

"Thank you."

"Mr. Lawson. Ms. Sinclair." He gave a short nod of his head and walked away and out the door.

"On a first-name basis," Justin said with a hint of sarcasm in his voice.

The elevator doors opened. They stepped aboard.

"What?"

"He called you Bailey."

She blinked in confusion, then it hit her. "I met him for the first time last night. He calmed me down when I got here and explained everything that was going on with my sister." She took his hand and looked into his eyes. "That's about it."

"Look, it's not a problem. I was wondering. That's all."

She linked her fingers through his. Her insides smiled. He was jealous.

The doors opened on the third floor, and they walked to the nurses' station to get Apryl's room number.

"I'll wait here. I don't want to walk in on your sister," Justin said. "She doesn't know me."

Bailey reached up and lightly kissed his lips. "Thanks." She hurried off down the corridor.

When she arrived at Apryl's room, she was up and dressed and sitting in a chair by the window.

"Sis." She smiled then winced.

"Hey." Bailey crossed the room. "How are you feeling?"

"Tired. Head hurts, and this cast and sling are annoying, but I'm here."

"I ran into Dr. Phillips, and you're all set to go home."

A nurse entered the room. "I have your discharge papers, Ms. Sinclair, and your prescriptions." She handed the papers to Apryl then turned to Bailey. "You'll be taking her home?"

"Yes."

"I'll get a wheelchair."

"I don't need one."

The nurse smiled. "Sorry. Hospital policy. I'll be right back."

Bailey sat on the edge of the bed. "I, uh, brought someone with me."

"Who? Addison?"

"No. A friend. His name is Justin."

"Oh, a man friend." She grinned. "Good for you, sis. It's about time."

Bailey made a face. "Anyway, we'll be taking his car to my place."

"His car? What happened to yours?"

She blew out a breath. "The short version…I had to get it towed. Finally conked out on me last night after I left here."

"Oh, damn. You need your ride."

"Yeah, I know."

"Sure can't use mine," she said and grimaced at the memory.

The nurse returned with the wheelchair and helped Apryl to sit. "You have all of your belongings?"

"Yes, thank you."

The nurse pushed Apryl out of the room and down the

corridor with Bailey right alongside. Justin rose from his seat as they approached.

"That's him?" Apryl whispered in awe.

"That's him."

"Yummy."

Justin joined the trio en route to the elevator.

"Justin, this is my sister Apryl."

The resemblance was remarkable. Apryl was a carbon copy of her older sister. Where Bailey kept her hair long, wiry and wild, Apryl's natural curls were cut close to her head. Bailey's more serious, worldly eyes were offset by Apryl's mischievous ones.

"Lucky lady," Justin said and hit her with his mega-watt smile.

"I don't always look like this," she joked. "Nice to meet you, though, and thanks for looking after my sister."

"It's been my pleasure to look after Bailey," he said on a deep note that stroked Bailey's insides with innuendo. He winked at Bailey, and her cheeks flushed.

They rode down in silence, and the nurse wheeled her out to the front. Justin went to get the car and when he pulled up in front of them, Apryl let out an expletive of shock and pleasure.

"Apryl," Bailey said in admonishment.

"What?" she innocently retorted.

The nurse helped her up while Justin grabbed his garment bag, jumped out and held open the passenger door. He helped her with her seat belt then walked around the other side to Bailey.

He stepped up close. "I'll call you later." He draped the garment bag over his shoulder and leaned down and kissed her slow and deep, letting his tongue play for a moment with hers. When he broke the kiss, Bailey felt light-headed. She blinked and slid her tongue across her bottom lip to savor the taste of him.

"Okay," she managed. "How are you going to get to the office?"

"I called a car service while I was waiting. It should be here in about ten minutes."

"Thank you…for everything."

"Whatever you need." He cupped her chin in his palm. "Whatever." He pecked her on the lips, turned and bent down to wave goodbye to Apryl then headed back inside, out of the heat, to wait for the car.

Bailey watched him until he blended in with the visitors and hospital staff then got in the car.

"Girl, you done hit a grand slam!"

"It's not like that, Apryl." She put the car in gear and eased away from the curb.

"If it's not, it should be."

Bailey turned on the music.

"So, spill. Where did you meet Mr. Fine?"

"At work."

"And?"

"And nothing. We're just friends."

"A friend with benefits." She laughed lightly.

Bailey shook her head. She wasn't going to feed into her sister's penchant for scintillating details. Apryl had no qualms about divulging her most intimate details about her various male friends, and believed that her sisters should reciprocate. Bailey didn't agree.

"Fine, don't tell," she said with a pout.

"I didn't intend to." A smile mirrored on her recently kissed lips.

"Does he have any brothers?"

"I haven't met his brother."

"How long have you known him? What does he do for a living to be able to afford this ride?"

"He's an attorney."

"Niiiice. Right up your alley. And speaking of right

up your alley, when do you start school? You are going back, aren't you?"

Bailey heaved a sigh. "I don't know." With so much going on in her life recently, she hadn't had a moment to focus on the upcoming fall semester. She still had no positive response for the grants and scholarships she'd applied for, and time was running out.

Then Apryl being Apryl zipped off topic to prattle on about the guy she'd met. Bailey half listened. She only wished she could be as carefree as her sister. But if she was, there was no telling where any of her siblings would be.

Chapter 14

By the time Justin arrived at his office building it was nearly one.

"You're pretty casual today, Mr. Lawson," his assistant teased.

"Hectic morning. Any messages?"

"A few." She handed him the slips of paper. "Mr. Hurley stopped by to see you. He asked that you give him a call when you get in."

"Thanks." He started for his office.

"Mr. Lawson…"

He stopped and turned. "Yes?"

"You have a three o'clock with Mr. Turner on his infringement case. Do you want to reschedule?"

"No. Thanks. Pull the files. We can meet in the small conference room."

"I already have it blocked for you from three to four."

"Hopefully it won't take that long," he said.

"I allowed for Mr. Turner's long-windedness." She smiled.

Justin went into his office and locked the door. He got out of his sweater and jeans and changed into his dark blue Italian-made business suit, winter-white shirt and pinstriped navy tie. He took his black wingtips from the bag and slid them on his feet. Reviewing his messages he decided that they all could wait until he'd spoken with Mr. Turner.

The afternoon sped by and true to form his client, Mr. Turner, took up the entire hour—all of which was billable.

Justin loosened his tie and put in a call to Carl, who told him that he'd gotten a call from the Realtor, and he had a place for them to look at that evening. Justin told him they'd have to ride together as Bailey had his car. Carl couldn't hide his shock knowing how much Justin loved that car. He'd never let anyone drive it—ever—not his siblings and not even him—his best friend.

"She got you whopped, my brother," Carl taunted.

"Call it whatever you want to call it. Just meet me out front at five-thirty."

Carl chuckled. "See you then."

Justin disconnected the call, sat back and gazed upward. Bailey Sinclair had certainly done something to him. Whatever it was, he liked it.

The space was located in Downtown Baton Rouge, about a mile away from their current office. It was a suite on the tenth floor, with space for reception and enough cubicle space for at least four employees with an additional two small offices.

"What do you think?" the Realtor asked once they'd completed the tour.

Justin exchanged a look with Carl. "It has everything that we're looking for. How long would the lease be?"

"We can do a one year or a two."

"How soon do you need an answer?" Carl asked.

"As soon as possible. Space in downtown is premium and rare, especially at this price."

Justin slung his hands into his pockets. "We'll get back to you first thing in the morning."

"Fair enough." He led them out and locked up.

"It's your call, man," Carl said as they pulled away from the building.

"I think it will suit our purposes as a start-up. We don't

need more space than this. I would have preferred a stand alone, but I think this will work."

"I'm down if you are."

Justin grinned. "Then I guess we go for it."

"I'll give him a call in the morning. I'm sure there'll be papers to sign."

"This is it, bro." Justin glanced at Carl.

"Yep, this is it.

"So let's hear it. What happened with Bailey?" Carl asked as he drove Justin home.

Justin brought him up-to-date on what had transpired up to him meeting Bailey's sister.

"Humph. You really dig this woman, don't you?"

Justin's smooth brows drew close. "Yeah, I really do."

"All I have to say on the subject is don't let the thrill of something new screw with your head. 'Cause let's be real. Bailey is not the type of woman you usually deal with. Your ready for all that?"

"Ready for what?"

"For bringing her into a world that…maybe she's not used to. You know the circles your family travels in."

"I can't believe you're saying this shit, man." His jaw tightened as he glared at Carl.

Carl held up one hand and kept the other on the wheel. "I'm being real. I'm not throwing shade on her. She is the exact opposite of every woman you've ever been with. That's the truth. So are you with her because she's different and you think you can 'rescue her' or is it real? I'm just asking. I wouldn't be a friend if I didn't bring it up."

Justin fumed, but there was some truth to what Carl said. Bailey was the polar opposite of every woman who'd slept in his bed. It *was* refreshing, and he *did* want to help her, do things for her. But he knew how she made him feel—truly alive in a relationship for the first time in his life. And he wanted more of it. He wanted more of her.

"I'll keep that all in mind," he grumbled. He and Carl

were always honest with each other, even if it pissed the other one off. He didn't have to admit that to Carl. It was an unspoken understanding.

They pulled up on Justin's street.

"You coming in for a minute?"

"Naw. I need to get home. Wife is waiting." He winked. "Talk to you tomorrow. You plan to call the Realtor or you want me to take care of it?"

"I'll give him a call when I get into the office. I have an 8:00 a.m. meeting, so I'll call when I'm done."

"Good. Then we can get the lease signed and get this show on the road."

They gave each other a fist bump and Justin got out. "Later."

Carl pulled off, and Justin headed inside, feeling truly inspired, and he wanted to share it with Bailey.

It was good having her sister with her. Apryl was truly entertaining with her tales of escapades with her line of suitors. She kept Bailey in stitches while she fixed them dinner. She checked the pot of jerk chicken that was simmering on the stove.

"Girl, you are a hot mess," Bailey said.

"You only live once, sis. I want to enjoy life and the men that come along with it. If I'm lucky, the right man will find me in the process."

Bailey caught the wistfulness in her voice. She looked at her. Apryl was staring off into the distance. Of all the children, Apryl had taken their mother's loss the hardest. She was the youngest and she'd needed a mother even more than her sisters, and with their father out of the picture and the string of men that their mother had brought home, Apryl grew up looking for love. She was still looking.

"A good man would be lucky to have you, Apryl. And probably when you stop looking…he'll find you." She gave her a warm smile.

"Like Justin found you?" She gave her sister a knowing look.

Bailey felt flush all over at the mention of his name. She turned away from the stove, wiped her hands on a towel then sat down at the shaky kitchen table. She blew out a breath. "He's…special. The way he makes me feel. But…"

"But what, sis?" Apryl reached her good hand across the table and covered her sister's clenched fist.

Bailey raised her gaze to her sister's questioning look. "It's so hard to explain. We come from two different worlds. Justin Lawson comes from one of the wealthiest families in Louisiana."

"And that's a bad thing, how?"

"You don't understand." She pushed up from the table.

"You're right, I don't."

"Every time I think about me and Justin…I think about mama and what happened with her."

Apryl's eyes searched her sister's face. "What really happened to Mom?"

Bailey lowered her head. "She chased after a dream… and believed that the right man could provide it for her…"

By the time Bailey finished telling Apryl about their mother, they were holding each other and shedding silent tears.

Bailey was cleaning up the kitchen when Justin called. "Hi."

"Hey, babe. How is everything?"

"Good. Just finished dinner. Apryl is resting, and I'm getting ready for work."

"I'll stop by the club. Have some things to tell you. Plus, I love to see you walking back and forth behind the bar."

Bailey giggled. "You are so bad."

"Oh, baby. I thought you told me I was so good." He chuckled.

"Bye, Justin."

"See you later, babe."

She hung up the phone with a big grin on her face then went to get ready for work.

"You sure you'll be okay?" she asked Apryl.

"I'll be fine." She yawned. "These pills will have me knocked out before you get to the front door."

"Okay, but call me if you need me."

"Mmm-hmm."

Bailey parked Justin's car and checked three times that it was locked before she went inside. Being responsible for that piece of beauty was nerve-racking to say the least. She didn't want anything to happen on her watch.

She pushed through the doors of Mercury and immediately felt the pulse of energy that flowed throughout the lavish space. She had to admit, Vincent had transformed what was once a three-story warehouse into one of the hottest spots in Baton Rouge. Every detail from the arrangement of the seating, the lights, private dining rooms, linens, live music, top-shelf liquor and mouthwatering cuisine to the hardworking and devoted staff combined to outshine every other club in the area. Although this was not her "dream job" she was happy to be part of the success and actually looked forward to coming to work. Not everyone could say the same thing. The only glitch in the program was the come-on by Vincent. That threw her for a loop and created a feeling of awkward tension—at least for her. Now, instead of seeking Vincent out for updates about Mercury and general conversation, she tried to avoid him, and it didn't feel good.

Bailey smiled and waved hello to the staff members that she passed on her way to her office. She had about fifteen minutes before she needed to hit her spot behind the bar, and she wanted to do a quick review of the weekly staffing schedule and the status of the private party.

She went into her office and closed the door behind

her, thankful that she hadn't run into Vincent in the narrow hallway. Quickly, she booted up her computer and reviewed the schedule and the arrangements for the private party. Everything looked good. The only item outstanding was the confirmed guest list for the party with several RSVPs still outstanding. The final head count would determine staffing. She hoped that the number would come in soon. She shut off her computer, locked her purse in her desk and stuck her cell phone into her pocket and headed out. Her luck was holding out, and she got to her station without running into Vincent.

"Hey, Mellie. How's it going?" She tied an apron around her waist.

"Busy." She grinned. "But what else is new on a Friday night? You have a particular glow about you," she said, looking Bailey up and down. "I bet it's that fine hunk that put a light in your eyes."

"Don't start, Mel."

"You can tell me, you know," she said, angling for information.

"I think a customer wants your attention," she said with a lift of her brow, unwilling to engage in conversation about her and Justin.

Mellie pouted. "Fine. Don't tell, but I say you hit paydirt landing a man like Justin Lawson." With that she sauntered down the length of the bar to a waiting customer.

Bailey blew out a breath and shook her head. *Paydirt.* Addy believed the same thing. But Bailey didn't want to entertain the idea that Justin was some meal ticket. For her it could never be that. She wouldn't allow it. Even if Justin could change her entire life and open her world to things she only read about, she wasn't going down that road. With that thought, the heartbreaking conversation she'd had with Apryl bloomed anew and reaffirmed her commitment to stand on her own. Period. Yet the unequal balance between her and Justin nipped at her conscience.

The steady flow of thirsty and hungry customers kept Bailey busy and totally focused on serving and entertaining those that sat in front of her. She felt on point tonight, exchanging barbs with some of the regulars and making newcomers feel welcomed enough that they would be sure to return. She'd spotted Vincent a few times from across the room, and her stomach tightened from the pensive looks he threw in her direction, but he didn't make any move to approach her.

It was nearing ten when Mellie sidled up to Bailey. "He's here," she teased, and gave Bailey a playful nudge with her elbow.

Bailey's heart jumped in her chest. She knew exactly who *he* was without looking because the tiny hairs on her arms had begun to tingle.

Slowly she turned around, and Justin was coming toward her. If she didn't know better she'd swear the seas parted as he strolled through the room with that confident swagger that only comes from one who knows exactly who they are and what they want. He was looking straight at her as if no one in the entire space existed.

Tonight he was totally casual. His black shirt had three buttons open and was tucked into expertly tailored black slacks, looped by a black lizard belt. He wore a diamond stud in his ear, something he left at home during office hours, and it picked up the light and gleamed against his smooth chocolate skin. He lifted his chin in greeting to Mellie and slid onto an available bar stool.

"Hey, babe," he whispered for only Bailey's ears.

She felt like some dumbstruck teen who'd met her rock-star idol.

"Hey." The smile was in her eyes. "Your usual?"

"Sounds good."

She turned away toward the shelf of bottles and went about preparing his drink, commanding herself to breathe and focus. She placed his glass of bourbon in front of him, and he intentionally brushed his fingers across hers. Electricity shot up her arm. She moaned.

"Dinner?" she whispered.

"I'll have plenty to eat when I take you home."

Her eyes widened for an instant.

Justin lifted the glass to his lips, and she envisioned what those lips could do to her.

"What do you think about that?"

The problem was she couldn't think, not with him burning a hole through her with his eyes. Her pulse quickened, and she didn't see Vincent until he was right beside her.

"I want you upstairs," he barked.

Bailey jerked back. "What?"

"I said I want you upstairs."

"Why? You have a staff up there and that will leave Mellie alone. We're busy."

He lowered his voice and stepped closer. "Last time I checked, this was my establishment. Let Steven know he should come down here."

Bailey's nostrils flared, and her skin burned with humiliation that Justin was a witness to her being dressed down.

"Fine." She couldn't look at Justin when she walked away. Her feet felt as if she was lifting them out of thick mud while she took the stairs to the upper level.

Unshed tears of humiliated frustration burned her eyes. She blinked them back, pasted on a smile and told Steven that he was needed on the main level. He was shocked but thrilled to have the chance to work the front lines. That's where all the action happened.

Bailey checked on the seated guests to ensure that their service was up to par then went behind the bar. She knew what Vincent was doing with this little stunt. He wanted to remind her that he could pull the plug whenever he wanted, and there wasn't anything that she could do about it. If she didn't need this job so badly, she would walk the hell out and tell Vincent exactly what he could do with himself. But she couldn't. All she could do for now was count the minutes until her shift was over.

Justin watched the entire exchange go down between Bailey and her boss with brewing fury. It took everything he had not to reach across the bar and grab that SOB by the collar and throw him onto the floor. He tossed back the remnants of his drink and paid his tab.

His dark eyes scanned the main floor. He spotted Vincent at the hostess podium. He glided off his seat and walked in that direction.

"I want to talk with you for a minute," he said, coming up behind Vincent.

Vincent turned and came face to chest with Justin. He looked up at the withering glare.

"Can I help you?"

"Why don't we step over here," Justin said with a tilt of his head that was away from the hostess.

Vincent pursed his lips. "Of course."

They stepped over to a quiet corner.

"I'm a friend of Bailey Sinclair. Justin Lawson."

"And…"

"Man to man. I know why you pulled Ms. Sinclair away from the bar. If you have a thing for Bailey, I can totally understand." His grin was nasty. "Man to man." He stepped closer. "She's taken. And you are not going to ever speak to her like that again."

A red flush began at Vincent's collar and raced to his cheeks. "Just who do you think you are coming into my establishment and telling me how to talk to my employees?"

"I already told you who I am, and I'd rather not have this conversation again—Vincent." His voice lowered to a mere rumble. "And I'm sure that Ms. Sinclair will have no further problems." With that he turned and left Vincent standing in place.

The hostess greeted him by name on his way out.

Vincent came up to her. "You know that man?"

She frowned. "Sure. Mr. Lawson. He comes in about two or three times a week. He's one of the Lawson heirs. Senator Lawson's son. Is there a problem, Vince? Did he complain about the service?"

He gritted his teeth. "No problem." He spun away and went directly to his office and shut the door. He turned on his computer and searched for Justin Lawson on Google. Almost instantly, a long list of articles and pictures were displayed about Justin Lawson.

Vincent clicked on the first link. It was an article about Justin Lawson, joining the law firm of Lake, Martin and DuBois, three years earlier. The article went on to detail his family tree and how the legacy of the Lawson name and brand would carry on as Justin was destined to move up the ranks in the legal world, having already made his mark on a major corporate case in his first six months at the firm.

Disgusted and infuriated, Vincent turned off the computer. Not only did Bailey have a man, but a man like Justin Lawson that could buy and sell him on a whim, too—one word from him and he could dry up Vincent's business.

Vincent wasn't a man used to feeling impotent. He worked too hard to get to where he was to have some privileged pretty boy millionaire ruin all that he'd accomplished—over a woman. Even if that woman was Bailey. Defeat wasn't an emotion that he'd ever had to deal with, but that's what he felt. Worse, if he didn't know before, he knew now that he'd never have a chance with Bailey.

"Bailey, what in the hell happened with you and Vincent?" Mellie asked in a harsh whisper when Bailey stopped to say good-night.

"Nothing. He just needed some help upstairs."

Mellie gave her a questioning look. "I didn't hear what he said, but I saw how he was talking to you. It didn't look friendly."

"Don't worry about it, Mel. Everything is fine." She forced a tight-lipped smile and made a move to leave.

"Well, it might have been *nothing* to you, but Justin didn't seem to take it too kindly."

Bailey stopped in her tracks. "What are you talking about?" Her heart began to race.

She gave a slight shrug. "He paid his bill right after you left, and I caught a glimpse of him and Vincent talking. That didn't look like a friendly conversation, either."

Bailey tried to beat back the thoughts that were running around in her head. If Justin… "See you tomorrow, Mel."

She stalked toward the exit with every manner of reprimand dancing on her tongue. What was it tonight with the humiliate Bailey routine? First Vincent and now Justin. She already had a good sense about Justin's take-charge attitude and his penchant for wanting to fix things. She and her life didn't need fixing!

Bailey pushed through the door with such force that it swung back and banged against the wall. Her eyes lit with anger when they landed on the Benz, reaffirming the undeniable truth of her position in her life. Her shoulders dropped. She blinked rapidly to stem the sting of tears building in her eyes. "Shit!"

And then, like all knights in shining armor, Justin was in front of her.

"Hello," he said tenderly, so sweet that her heart felt like it was fracturing into a million brilliant pieces.

Her throat tensed and whatever she wanted to spew at him clung there, held back by the gentleness in his eyes and in his touch as he stroked her chin.

"You okay?"

She could only nod, afraid that her voice wouldn't respond.

"Sure?"

"I am now," she managed.

He let his finger trail along the curve of her jaw. "Do you need to go home? To see about your sister?"

He was giving her an out if she needed to take it, and the realization softened her even more.

"Apryl said the pain meds knock her out." Her gaze lifted to meet his magnetic one, and it drew her closer. "She said she would sleep through the night."

"Perfect." He leaned in and stroked her lips with his, sending a shiver of need through her limbs.

"Follow me home," he said against her mouth.

"Okay."

"I'm parked across the street. Black Navigator."

She spotted it.

Justin crossed the street. The alarm chirped, and he got in. The headlights illuminated the street—the path that she couldn't seem to resist taking. She drew in a steady breath, got into the Benz and pulled off behind Justin.

Chapter 15

"Make yourself comfortable. I'll fix us a drink. Wine or something stronger?"

Bailey put her purse on the side table. "Wine. Please."

"Yes, ma'am."

Bailey took off her shoes and tucked her legs beneath her. Once again, she slowly took in the understated opulence of how Justin and his family lived. It was a lifestyle that had always been out of her reach. And now she could touch it. She could reach out and wrap her fingers around it. Her stomach fluttered. It would be so easy to simply give in.

"Here you go."

She blinked. Justin handed her the glass of wine.

"Thanks."

He sat down beside her. She took a sip and sighed with pleasure.

"Love that sound."

Her lids fluttered open. She looked at him. "What sound?"

"That purring sound that you make in the back of your throat."

Warmth flowed through her as Justin teased the fine hairs at the back of her neck with his fingertips. If he kept this up, she would come all over herself.

"I didn't…realize I did that."

"There is a long list of things that you do that make me crazy." He angled his body toward hers. "Like the way that tiny pulse flutters in your throat when I get close to you, or the way your lips move, the sway in your hips, the way you pour my drinks, the light that sparks in your eyes when you talk about the law, your laughter, the huskiness in your voice, the brilliance of your mind, the way you move under me when we make love." His jaw tightened. "The list is long."

Her chest rose and fell in rapid succession as she tried to breathe. No one had ever spoken to her like that. No man had ever made her feel that she was more than a nice time before moving on. Most couldn't deal with the luggage that she carried around with her—the responsibility that she felt for her siblings. Would Justin feel the same way once he knew the entire story?

Justin sensed that his "confession" had made her uncomfortable. It wasn't his intention. He took a sip of his drink. "Hungry?"

She grinned. "Starved."

He got up and took her hand, pulling her to her feet. "I know about some of your talents, Ms. Sinclair. Let's see how you do in the kitchen."

"Oh, baby, don't even go there. I get down in the kitchen."

"You're on."

Bailey took a look in the fridge and cabinets. In short order she'd diced and sliced all the ingredients for a Food Network–worthy omelet, stuffed with spinach, cheddar cheese, shrimp, peppers and spices and cooked light as cotton. She cut up strawberries, kiwi and melon slices and placed them in two small bowls. Then she fixed them both mimosas to go with their late-night, early morning feast.

"Well?" she asked after Justin had taken his first mouthful.

"Babe…your case…is rested." He picked up another fork of food and chewed with relish. He pointed his fork toward her self-satisfied grin. "You have skills."

Bailey giggled. "This is light work. One day maybe I'll cook a *real* meal for you."

"You're on." He tasted the mimosa. "Good stuff. Not my usual, but good. Goes down well with the meal."

"Of course," she joked. "It's what I do." She focused on her plate and then popped a strawberry in her mouth.

Justin watched the shift in her demeanor when she mentioned what she did. He knew where it stemmed from. He wouldn't push it. But if that piece of work calling himself her boss gave her any more grief, he would have a real problem.

"Hey, we found a location today."

"You did? Where?"

"Downtown. Nice office spaces. Exactly what we need for now. We should sign the lease this week."

Bailey beamed. "Congratulations. That's wonderful. Big step. This makes it real."

"Yep."

She scooted her chair closer and covered his hand with hers. "I'm really happy for you. There's no greater feeling than seeing your dreams materialize."

"I want to make a difference."

"You will."

He leaned in and kissed her, tasting the sweetness of the strawberries on her lips. He wanted more. He lifted a strawberry from his bowl and put it on the tip of his mouth and came to her. She parted her lips and bit down. The sweet juice dribbled over their lips. She sucked the rest into her mouth, and Justin went after it, delving into her mouth with his hungry tongue.

Bailey moaned, and the sound incited him. He threaded his fingers through her tight mass of curls and pulled her to him. Tongues and lips tasted and suckled and danced in and out. He nibbled her bottom lip, and electricity sparked through her. Justin ran his hands down the column of her spine, and her body arched toward him. Her nipples hardened to tight pebbles, and she wanted to free them from the maddening sensation of them brushing against her bra.

He knew what she wanted. He unbuttoned her blouse, and a groan rose from the pit of his belly when the soft full flesh made an appearance. He buried his face between the swell of her breasts then ran his tongue along the deep valley. He cupped her breasts in his palms and lifted them higher, nuzzling the delicate fabric away until he could take the pleading nipple into his mouth.

Bailey cried out.

Justin tugged her shirt off and tossed it aside. His dark eyes deepened as they scorched across her face and down along her lush body as he slowly disrobed her. He reached into the bowl and picked a piece of kiwi, squeezed the juice along her skin then licked it away.

Prickly heat raced along her flesh. Her head spun from the thrill, the growing need. His hands and mouth seemed to be everywhere at once. She was on fire. She fumbled with the buckle of his slacks, unzipped and freed him. His groan intensified the heat that roared through her. She held him in her palm, stroked him, felt him grow and throb.

Justin pushed her black panties aside and found her slick welcome. He fingered her and felt her entire body shudder.

"You feel so good," he groaned hot in her ear. He lifted her as if she weighed no more than a loaf of bread and pushed her up against the refrigerator. Bailey locked her long legs around his back.

"Ahhhhh," she cried out when he pushed deep inside her and buried her face in the hollow of his neck.

Justin's muscles tensed as the thrill of feeling her envelop him raced through him. "So good," he groaned as he moved in and out of her.

"More," she whispered, pressing her fingers into his back.

He tightened his hold on her rear, kneading the firm

flesh and plunged deeper, harder, faster until the only sounds in the kitchen were the slapping of skin against skin and their moans that rose and fell in a chorus of ecstasy.

After, they stumbled laughing and naked up to his bedroom and tumbled onto his bed. Bailey draped her damp body across Justin's. She placed tiny kisses across the expanse of his chest.

Justin held her, feeling her heart beat hard and steady against him. He hadn't expected to feel this way so soon, so fast, about anyone. But the more he was with her, the more he wanted, and he would do whatever he must to make that happen.

"I know you said something to Vincent," she whispered into the darkened room.

He stroked her back.

"You didn't have to. I can handle Vincent."

"He's not going to talk to you like that. No one is. Not when I'm in your life."

Bailey sat up, made out his face. "I don't need you to come to my rescue, Justin."

He rose up and balanced his weight on his elbow. Her body was outlined by the moonlight. "What kind of men are you used to, Bailey? The kind that sit back and let things happen to the woman they care about? I'm not that man."

She turned her head.

"Look at me."

"Is that really the kind of man you want? Because that's not what you deserve."

Her features tightened. "You don't understand."

"No. I don't, so tell me. Be honest with me."

Her mouth worked, but no words came out.

He reached out to her, held her arm. "Talk to me, babe."

"My mother committed suicide when I was twenty-seven. Never knew who or where our father was." Her throat tightened. "He could have been any number of men that came in and out of our lives." She sniffed and was glad for the darkness that masked the shame in her eyes.

Justin gently squeezed her arm, stroked her thigh.

"I had just started law school but after two years, I had to drop out to get a job to take care of my siblings, so I put my dreams of continuing law school on hold."

"That was quite a sacrifice for you," he said in admiration.

She uttered an abbreviated laugh. "I had no other choice."

"Tell me about your siblings," he quietly urged.

She tugged in a breath. "My younger sister Tory is under the misconception that she was destined to live the high life, no matter the cost. And my baby sister, Apryl, humph, there isn't a man that misses her radar..." Bailey sighed heavily. "It's hard to keep them on track."

"And all the weight fell on you."

"Yeah. I had to take care of them. I still do. They depend on me."

"I'm no psychologist but it sounds like your mother's life and death affected each of you the same way."

"The same way?"

"Yeah, everyone is looking for something to fill the loss. Including you."

She vigorously shook her head. "No."

"Think about it."

She pushed up from the bed. "Don't you get it, Justin? I don't want to think about it. I don't want to talk about it anymore, either." She stalked off to the bathroom and solidly shut the door behind her.

Justin tucked his hands beneath his head and stared into the dark room. There was more to the story, that much he knew for sure. The feelings that he had for Bailey only deepened by her revelations. She may not need him or want him to *rescue* her, but he felt deep in his gut that it was exactly what she needed—to be truly loved—the way he wanted to love her.

His insides jerked as if shocked. *Love.* Was he falling in love with Bailey? He glanced toward the closed bathroom door. He was in it to find out.

Chapter 16

They didn't talk anymore that night about her past, the thing that haunted her. They talked about little things, the getting-to-know-you things, how she got to be a bartender, what it felt like being the youngest Lawson, places they'd been, favorite lines from movies. Those kinds of things that couples finding their way to each other talk about.

"You all set up for school for the fall?"

"Hmm, it's coming together."

"I know you don't want to hear this, but if you want me to make a couple of calls…"

"No, Justin."

"All right. All right. All right," he said in a pretty damned good imitation of Matthew McConaughey, that made her burst out laughing. He kissed the back of her neck, and she spooned closer.

"Do you have plans for tomorrow?"

"Spending the day with you, if you let me." He kissed her again.

"I'd like that."

"Yeah, me, too." He held her closer, and they drifted off to sleep.

Bailey awakened and found herself alone in the massive bed. She rubbed the sleep out of her eyes and languidly stretched. Everything ached in a good way, and it brought a smile to her face thinking about why she felt the way she did.

She heard Justin's voice coming from downstairs, and another male voice. What time was it? She checked the bedside clock. It was after ten.

"Damn." At least she didn't have to tiptoe downstairs in search of her clothes. Justin must have brought them up while she was asleep. She scrambled to get dressed. Apryl was definitely up by now, and she must be worried. She checked her phone for messages. There was only one from Addison, calling to see if she wanted to catch a movie before her shift.

Her shift. Her stomach rolled. She had no idea what Justin said to Vincent, and she didn't want to know. But what she was certain of was that Justin made himself clear to Vincent. And she had a strong feeling that Vincent wouldn't be giving her a hard time going forward. As much as she didn't want to, it gave her a little thrill to know that Justin dealt with Vincent—for her.

Bailey gazed into the mirror, studying her reflection. She looked exactly the same, but something inside her was changing. Justin's laughter rose up the staircase. It was because of him, and she wasn't sure if she could stop it, or if she wanted to.

Bailey came downstairs and followed the sound of voices that led her to the living room.

"Hey, babe." Justin rose from the arm of the side chair and came up to her. He placed a hand on her hip. "Hope we didn't wake you," he said quietly while his eyes scanned her face.

"No. I needed to get up." She inhaled his intoxicating scent, and that crazy need for him began to simmer.

Justin stepped closer, blocking her from his guest. "I want you…" He placed a light kiss on her forehead, took her hand and turned around. "You remember Carl. He was with me the night we met." Justin led her fully into the room.

Bailey couldn't think straight after that sexual gauntlet that he'd just thrown.

Carl stood. "Good to see you again."

Bailey remembered to smile. "You, too."

"I told Carl that I owe him big-time.

Bailey glanced at him. "Why?"

Justin slipped his arm around her waist. "If he hadn't insisted that I come to the Mercury Lounge that night and then told me to stay after he had to leave, we would have never met." He kissed her full on the lips, lingering for a moment before guiding her over to the couch.

Bailey felt so off balance, unaccustomed to public displays of affection directed at her. But as she was quickly coming to understand, that's the kind of man Justin was—ready to take a stand and have his position made clear.

"We were going to play a quick game of tennis out back while you go and check on your sister. I can swing by and get you about one—then we'll find something to do. How's that sound?"

"Great. I'll be ready."

"There's coffee and tea in the kitchen, and there's a plate for you on the warming tray. I'd love to take credit, but our housekeeper fixed everything."

It was awkward enough that she had to do the "morning-after walk" in front of Carl, but the housekeeper knew she was there, too.

"Tough life this brotha has," Carl teased.

"Very funny." He turned to Bailey. "I'll get your plate." He walked off before she could protest.

Bailey eased over to the club chair and sat. "So… Justin's been telling me about the venture."

"Yeah, he's been talking and working on this for a couple of years. His father wanted him to go the corporate route and eventually follow in his political footsteps. It's a major bone of contention between them. But Justin went along with the whole working-in-a-law-office thing for as long as he could—to make his father happy, but his heart was never in it. For a man who has everything, all he's ever wanted to do was help others. Now he has that chance."

Bailey's heart softened even more hearing about Justin from Carl.

"You've made quite an impression on him."

Her eyes flicked toward Carl. "I have?"

"Definitely. To be honest, you're not the type of woman he usually dates. Don't get me wrong. It's just that in the circles that his family travels in—there are a lot of *takers*—for lack of a better word. All surface and no substance. From everything he's told me about you—you're nothing like them, and it's what he's been looking for."

"What who's been looking for?" Justin placed Bailey's plate on a lap tray and gave it to her. "What lies has he been telling you?"

"Oh, my," she said, taking in the cheese grits, turkey sausage, eggs and fruit. "This is too much."

"Eat what you want," Justin said offhandedly.

She smiled up at him. "Thank you."

"Anything you need," he said only for her ears.

"We were talking about The Justice Project," Bailey said and shot Carl a conspiratorial look. She took a spoonful of fruit and had a momentary flashback of the night before.

"Carl is going to stay with the firm for a while until we're fully operational."

"Yes, my lovely wife has grown very accustomed to a comfortable lifestyle." He chuckled. "Happy wife, happy life. As a matter of fact, you should bring Bailey to the house for dinner. Gina always wants to have a reason to lay out a spread."

"He's right about that," Justin added.

"Besides, maybe once she meets Bailey, she'll stop trying to play matchmaker."

Justin looked down at Bailey. "I've definitely stopped

looking," he said quietly. "Let us know when," which was as much a statement as a question.

"I'd like that," Bailey said. She took a sip of orange juice.

"Probably after the fund-raiser," Carl said. "Gina is on the committee, so I know she's busy until then."

"Right." Justin arched his neck back. "Totally forgot about that." He sat down on the arm of Bailey's chair. "It's a pretty big deal, and I want you to go with me." His voice lowered. "So I can show you off."

Bailey swallowed back the rise of anxiety that bubbled up from her stomach. She'd never been to any foundation fund-raiser and could only imagine the glitz and glamour that she could never match.

Justin registered the hesitation in her eyes. "We'll talk about it, and you let me know," he said, gallantly giving her a way out. "I know how crazy your schedule is."

"I'll let you know."

He leaned down and kissed her forehead. "Whatever you want, babe."

Her throat burned with unspoken emotion. He *understood.* She gave him a smile of thanks. "And speaking of stuff to do…" She placed the tray with her half-eaten food on the table. "I've really got to go." She stood. "Thank your housekeeper for me."

Carl rose from his seat, and Bailey realized how tall he was. He had Justin's six feet three inches beat by at least two inches. The two friends cut an imposing figure. He extended his hand.

"I'll be looking forward to seeing you again."

"Me, too. Take care."

Justin walked her to the door. "Sorry we couldn't have the morning to ourselves. I'd forgotten about the tennis game." He leaned against the frame of the door, folded his arms and sucked her in with his gaze. "Seems like I'm forgetting a lot of things lately."

"Why is that?" she asked, a bit breathless.

Dark orbs traversed her upturned face. "Because you're all I think about."

Bailey's heart thumped. Her breath hitched as he lowered his head and kissed her with an intensity that made her knees weaken. She gripped the tight ropes of his arms.

"Mmm, sure you have to go? I can get rid of Carl," he murmured, pulling her tight against his arousal.

She gasped. "I can't…"

Justin drew in a tight breath and reluctantly stepped back. "I will see you later."

"Definitely." She raised up and pecked him on the lips then quickly turned in time to avoid him snatching her back.

Her laughter brightened the late-morning air.

Justin watched her until she'd left the driveway before returning to Carl, which also gave him some time to tame the tiger.

"I like her," Carl said when Justin came back. "Something genuine about her." He finished off his orange juice. "I'm happy for you, man."

A wistful grin lifted the corner of his mouth. "I like her, too. More than I thought I would. And you're right. She does make me happy. Happier than I've been for a while." *If only she'd let me get past some of the walls she's put up*, he thought.

Chapter 17

Bailey jogged up the three flights of stairs to her apartment with the spring and bounce of a teenager.

Apryl was up and resting on the couch. A pang of guilt thumped in Bailey's chest. She had been so involved with her and Justin that she'd totally neglected to think about the help that Apryl would need just to fix something to eat or bathe or get dressed.

"Sis, I'm so sorry. I should have been here when you got up." She tossed her purse onto the table and went straight to the kitchen sink to wash her hands. She dried her hands on a dish towel and pulled open the fridge. "What do you want to eat? I have eggs, bacon—"

"I'm not hungry," she said petulantly.

Bailey spun around. She leaned against the sink and folded her arms. *Here we go.* "What's the problem, Apryl?"

"*You* asked me to come here," she snapped, rocking her neck as she spoke. "*You* said you would take care of me. *You* didn't even bother to call. *You* didn't know if I was dead or alive."

"Apryl...really?" She tilted her head to the side and squinted at her sister, who actually had the nerve to pout. "What did you say to me before I left last night?"

"This is what Mom would do!" She threw a side glare at Bailey. "Just leave us...for some man."

Bailey rocked back on her heels as if she'd been pushed in the chest. Her gaze fell on the pile of the unpaid bills that mirrored her own dreams put on hold and the half life she lived because she'd always put her family first—above herself—wanting to be for them everything that their mother had never been. She'd mistakenly believed that in finally telling Apryl the truth about their mother, Apryl would realize what she'd been trying to do all these years.

A pain that she had no name for opened up inside her. She felt ill. Addison's words of wisdom about her family echoed in her head.

"Sorry you feel that way." She tossed the dish towel across the counter and walked off to her bedroom.

Bailey sat down hard on the edge of her bed. She'd spent years of her adult life looking out for her siblings: coming to the rescue, covering finances, providing refuge, being the sounding board for their woes. And for what? A rude and painful awakening. An awakening that had always been there but she'd refused to see it. She had no choice but to see it now.

She stripped out of her clothes and tossed them in the hamper then turned on the shower full blast until the room filled with steam. She stepped beneath the beat of the shower, letting the water pelt her skin as the sting of her tears flowed down the drain.

The sound of one of the midday talk shows filtered into her room. It sounded like that doctor that Oprah made famous. For a moment Bailey saw herself in the guest seat surrounded by her siblings and wondered what sage advice the good doctor would have for her. How many hours of counseling would the Sinclair family need?

Bailey fastened the button on her black jeans and pulled a black fitted T-shirt over her head, dug in her top dresser drawer and pulled out a burned-orange-and-gold oblong scarf. She piled her hair on top of her head and then fashioned the scarf into a headband. She added a pair of silver hoop earrings and then threaded a silver-toned belt through the loops of her jeans.

All the little details of getting ready to go out with Justin kept her mind off what Apryl had said. Almost.

She leaned closer to the mirror to coat her lashes with mascara, and as she looked into her reflection, she wondered if her other sister saw her the same way that Apryl did.

Bailey straightened, drew in a steadying breath and turned away from the truth. She barely heard the faint *ping-pong* of the downstairs doorbell cut through the sound of applause coming from the television; a sure sign of another successful intervention from the good doctor. She glanced at her watch. It wasn't even twelve thirty. It couldn't be Justin. She walked barefoot to the front of the apartment, but Apryl had already buzzed the door.

"Who was that?"

Apryl shrugged. "I thought I pressed Talk but I guess I pressed Door. She plopped down on the couch and winced from the impact.

Bailey huffed and shook her head in concert with the knock on her apartment door. She peered through the peephole. Justin. Damn it. She'd intended to meet him downstairs. She opened the door and as tense and off balance as she felt, the sensations began to dissipate when she looked into Justin's eyes and watched the heart-melting smile illuminate the space around them.

"Hey."

"Hey yourself."

"I know I'm a little early. I made quick work of whipping Carl's ass so that you and I could spend more time together."

Bailey grinned. "Humble, aren't we."

"When you got it, you got it." He winked.

Well, she couldn't stand there in the doorway making small talk. He'd have to see where and how she lived at some point. She took his hand. "Come on in. I need some shoes." She glanced down at her bare feet.

"Yep. I would say so."

Bailey led him inside.

"Apryl, hello. How are you feeling?" He came over and sat next to her on the couch.

Bailey hesitated for a moment then went to her room. The quicker she got ready, the better.

"Coming along," Apryl said.

"You had your sister really worried. We're glad that you're okay. Listen—" he lowered his voice "—I wanted to thank you."

"For what?"

"For hanging tough last night. Bailey needed some downtime. She's been dealing with a lot lately." He flashed that smile.

Apryl's stiff demeanor softened. "It's not a problem. I told her she needs to enjoy herself. The pain pills had me in la-la land anyway."

"I still wanted to thank you."

"Ready," Bailey announced.

Justin pushed up from his spot next to Apryl. "You take it easy. When you're up to it maybe we can all do something together."

"Three's a crowd."

"Never. You're Bailey's sister. Family."

Apryl's gaze drifted toward her sister.

Bailey's chest tightened. She didn't want to believe that she saw regret in her sister's demeanor. It was what she wanted but not what she expected.

Justin draped his arm across Bailey's shoulders, and they walked out.

"Everything okay?" he asked while he opened the door to the Navigator.

"Yes. Fine. Why?" She hopped up inside, and Justin shut the door.

He got in behind the wheel and secured his seat belt then turned on the ignition. "Because things seemed kind of strained between you and your sister." When Bailey only looked straight ahead, he continued. "Am I wrong?"

"Not entirely."

"You want to talk about it?"

She shook her head. "Not now. Maybe later."

Justin studied her profile. He was used to sibling squabbles. Growing up in a house full of strong-willed, opinionated people, conflict was inevitable. This was something different. For now he'd leave it alone. Bailey was as stubborn as he was. She'd tell him when she was ready.

"So," she said, shoving cheer into her voice. "Where are we going?"

"Thought I'd drive us down to the pier and we could board the Ole Miss for the midday cruise. How's that sound?"

Bailey beamed a genuine smile. "I've always wanted to do that."

"You mean you're a born and raised Louisiana girl and you've never been on Ole Miss?"

"Nope."

"That ends today. As a matter of fact, I'm going to make it my mission to take you to all the places you've wanted to go but have never been."

Bailey adjusted her body toward him. They stopped at a light.

"Why?" she whispered.

Justin frowned. "Why what?"

"Why do you do what you do for me?" She needed him to look her in the eye. She needed to know that it was more than just sex, more than simply taking a walk on the other side, more than one of his projects that he thought he could fix.

"Can't it simply be because I care about you, really care about you? I want to see you smile. I want to see the light in your eyes when you're excited. I want you to be happy."

"What makes you think I'm not happy or that I need you or any man to make me happy?"

His features constricted as if struck with a sudden pain, but she couldn't stop the words that continued to flow.

"Men always think that the poor, helpless woman needs the big strong man to rescue her from her mundane life." Flashes of the numerous "uncles" ran through her head. "I don't. I'm not one of those women." She wasn't like her mother.

Bailey watched his jaw tighten and his fingers grip the steering wheel.

"For what it's worth, Bailey, I'm not one of those men," he said quietly.

The midday cruise on Ole Miss was strained to say the least. They made small talk about the weather, avoided eye contact and murmured about the cuisine.

The drive back home to her apartment was more awkward than the past couple of hours.

Justin kept his eyes on the road and hummed tunelessly along to the music coming from the speakers as if she wasn't there. She couldn't blame him.

Bailey knew she'd gone too far. She'd intentionally hurt him when that unnamed fear put those words into her mouth, even though deep in her soul she knew she had nothing to fear from Justin. But that didn't stop the phantom of her past from materializing.

They pulled up in front of her apartment building. Justin popped open the lock from the panel on his armrest.

"Safe and sound."

Bailey focused on her entwined fingers. "Thanks. The cruise was great."

Justin didn't respond.

Bailey reached for the door handle, stopped, glanced over her shoulder then opened the door and got out. The Navigator pulled off before she could reach her front step.

Chapter 18

"**Y**ou said what?" Addison ground out from between her teeth, practically leaping over the bar in the process.

Bailey pushed Addison's mimosa in front of her. "I know. I know." She ran her fingers through her twist of curls.

The Mercury Lounge was relatively quiet. Bailey was grateful for that. It was hard to concentrate with flashes of her crazy rant at Justin running through her head. When Addison had called her earlier, she couldn't keep the ache out of her voice that Addison easily picked up on. Addison was insistent on coming straight to Bailey's apartment, but Bailey didn't want Apryl to overhear anything. She still had Apryl's revelation to deal with, but it stung too much at the moment. She knew if she talked to her sister with the mental space that she was in, she'd say something to Apryl that she wouldn't be able to take back. So she'd finally agreed to talk with Addison at the bar.

Addison took a swallow of her drink. "What would make you say something like that?"

Bailey slowed her busy work of wiping the bar top and gripped the edge with her fingertips. "I'd gotten into a thing with Apryl." She replayed the conversation.

"That little ungrateful…" She held up her hand to stop herself. "I know she's your sister, but give me five minutes with her in the bathroom."

Bailey laughed for the first time in hours. "Addy, you need to stop."

"Humph, you think I'm joking." She rolled her eyes. "So instead of enjoying your afternoon with that fine specimen of a man, you jump all over him instead of Apryl."

"Something like that," she admitted.

"That's only part of it."

Bailey's gaze rose to meet Addison's all-seeing one. "What do you mean?"

"You know what I mean. The instant anyone gets close to you, you get radioactive." She touched Bailey's fingers. "At some point you've got to stop being afraid that to allow yourself to love, to open your heart, that you're going to turn into your mother."

Bailey's nostrils flared. "You don't know what you're talking about."

"Don't I? I'm your friend, B. Your best friend. I've been hip to hip with you through all the bull. So, yeah, I do know. At some point you're going to have to step out of Phyllis's shadow and walk in your own light."

"I heard myself," she said in a faraway voice. "I heard the words. I saw what they were doing, and I couldn't stop myself. I wanted to hurt him…"

"Before he hurt you."

Bailey blinked back the water in her eyes.

"The way I see it, you can chalk this up and blow maybe the best thing that's happened to you in a while, or you can take your ass over there and be honest with him—about everything. If he can't deal then it wouldn't have worked anyway. But if he can—" she looked into Bailey's eyes "—happiness is waiting for you."

Justin stepped out of the shower and draped a towel around his waist. He used a hand towel to wipe away the steam on the mirror. He examined his reflection. He could see the hard line of his father's jaw and the warmth of his mother's eyes. His mother would be proud of what he'd accomplished and would have been rooting for his success with The Justice Project. His father, on the other hand, grudgingly accepted his decision to leave the firm while at the same time reminding him that he was ruining his career. It would always be difficult for his father and his uncles to understand and accept that their children were just as stubborn and driven as they were, and that they'd carve their own paths.

Justin ran his hand across his chin. A quick shave was in order. He plugged in his electric shaver and turned it on just as his cell phone began to dance and vibrate on the sink. Bailey's name and image appeared on the face. He let it ring, watching her face smile back at him. He'd taken that picture the night of the concert. Things certainly had changed since then. He pressed the green talk icon.

"Hello."

"Justin, it's me, Bailey," she said inanely.

"I know."

He wasn't going to make this easy, but she refused to be discouraged. "I wanted to talk with you about today, the things I said."

"Not sure what there is to say, Bailey. You were pretty clear."

She squeezed her eyes shut. "I know you think I was, but you don't have all the facts, counselor. Before you make a decision…don't you want to hear all of the evidence?"

Justin's mouth flickered in a grin. "I'm listening."

"I'm outside."

"Excuse me?" He tightened the towel around his waist and walked out of the bathroom.

"I'm in front of your house. The things I need to say need to be said face-to-face."

Justin jogged down the stairs to the main level, looked out the front window. The headlights of his Benz spread softly against the driveway. His mama always said it was ungentlemanly to keep a lady waiting.

He went to the front door and pulled it open. For a moment his towel-clad body was framed by the beam of the car's headlights. Bailey turned off the car, and the space around them dipped into a silhouette of intimacy.

She knew without a doubt that he had nothing on beneath the towel, and his bare chest only made it more difficult for her to concentrate on what she'd come to say. His body blocked her way, forcing her to stare at him. Her breathing escalated, and for a moment she thought he might not let her in.

Justin finally stepped aside to let her pass then shut the door with a thud. "Have a seat. I'm going to put something on."

Bailey wanted to tell him that he was fine just the way he was, but she held her tongue.

Too nervous to sit, she slowly paced the expansive space then walked over to the glass doors that opened onto the pool and the grounds that appeared to go on forever. This was the life, the world he lived in, and she wasn't sure that she could ever be a part of it. But she wanted him. She wanted Justin, and somehow she was going to have to convince him of that and let go of her past.

"Can I get you something?"

Bailey turned toward the sound of the voice that she heard in her dreams, and her breath caught at the sight of him.

Yes, he'd gotten out of the towel, only to put on a pair of low-riding drawstring sweats that drew the eye to the rock-hard abs and the thin trail of hair that led to hours of pleasure. She tore her eyes away.

"Um, some water is fine."

He went into the kitchen and returned shortly with a glass of water with ice, handed it to her then went to lean against the mantel. "So…what do you want to talk about?"

"First…I'm sorry. I shouldn't have lashed out at you. It has nothing to do with you. You were just the recipient of all the stuff that I've been dealing with." She swallowed. Justin hadn't moved; his expression hadn't changed. "I was the one that…found my mother. I'd come home from school—first year of law school. I'd stopped off after class to the law library then a local diner. I knew I was stalling. I didn't want to go home." She had a distant smile. "It was October tenth. Around five. It was already getting dark. The apartment was quiet. I figured my sisters were at friends' houses." She took a swallow of water.

"I went to my room, and that's when I saw water coming out from under the bathroom door. The first thing I thought was that my lazy sister Tory had left the water running. I…I didn't expect…to find my mother in the tub. She'd cut her wrist and taken some pills. There was water and blood, and I started screaming. I tried to wake her. I did CPR…" She shook her head at the vision. "It was too late."

"Bailey…"

She held up her hand. She had to get it out now, or she never would. "My mother struggled for years to feed and clothe us and keep a roof over our heads when my father left her and us—we were too young to even remember him. My mother was beautiful." She smiled wistfully. "Men flocked to her beauty, and she believed that was all she needed. She discovered that she could use her looks to get men to give her things, to pay for things, to keep her company. So the 'uncles' started to come and go. But they would tire of her looks, tire of her neediness, tire of her three kids." She took another sip of water. "She spent her days trying to catch that man that was going to take care of her, but they all eventually abused her emotionally, and then they were gone." Tears streamed down her cheeks.

"I tried to protect my sisters from seeing stuff. I made excuses for the times when Mom wouldn't come out of her room or when she would disappear for days at a time and leave us alone." She sniffed hard then swiped at her eyes. "After…I had to drop out of school, get a job to take care of them. I had to be there…" She lowered her head.

Justin crossed the distance between them and gathered her into his arms. "I can see how hard you try to be strong and independent at the expense of your own happiness. It's okay to need someone, Bailey. I don't want to take away your independence, babe." He stepped back a bit and lifted her chin so that she would have to look at him. "I only want you to be happy."

"Sometimes I feel like I'm failing my sisters."

"Bailey, there comes a point in everyone's life when they have to take responsibility for their own choices and stop using the past as an excuse for their future. Your siblings are all adults. What happened with your mom was horrible, and it affected each of you in a different way. But you can't blame yourself, and you can't save people who don't know they need to be saved."

She wiped her eyes. "I've been told that a zillion times by Addy."

Justin grinned. "Smart girl."

"She thinks so, too." She exhaled a long breath. "My head tells me all of that is true. It's my heart that keeps getting in the way."

Justin slung his hands in his pockets. "You may not want to hear this, but I'm going to take a chance and say it anyway. You still feel guilty."

She frowned. "Guilty? About what?"

"That you didn't come straight home that day. That if you had come home, you could have saved her."

The air caught in her chest. Her temples began to pound. She'd never told anyone, not even Addy that she was late getting home that day. She'd never said it out loud. Her shoulders shook as the sobs overtook her.

Justin held her, stroked her hair, her back, cooed softly that it was okay; she would be okay.

Bailey sank into the security of his arms and his words.

All this time, guilt had been the phantom that stalked her. It was the voice in the recesses of her subconscious. She blamed herself, but even understanding that didn't make the guilt go away.

"Let me fix you something a little stronger." He kissed her forehead and walked her over to the couch. "Thank you for telling me," he said as he fixed her a shot of scotch and him a bourbon. He sat beside her and handed her the glass. He touched his glass to hers. "To getting over the hurdles…together."

Bailey's smile trembled around the edges. She took a sip of her drink and hummed as the heat of the honey-brown liquid flowed down her throat and ignited in her belly. She knew her liquors, and this was definitely the good stuff. Of course, she wouldn't expect anything less from Justin.

"I didn't tell you all of that for you to feel sorry for me."

Justin bit back a smile. "I know." He put his arm around her shoulder. "You make it very difficult to feel sorry for you."

Bailey made a face. "I told you about my family, tell me about yours, stuff that's not in the papers."

"Well, this is family news. My oldest sister, Lee Ann, is expecting twins!"

"Wow. How exciting."

"Second set of twins in the family. Desi and Dom thought they had a lock on it." He chuckled. "I'm sure you've heard about my brother, Rafe."

"I've seen a couple of pictures of him. You two look a lot alike."

"Yeah, he swears he's the better-looking one, but you and I both know that's a lie." He winked.

"You are absolutely right."

"Anyway, Rafe is off in Europe, playing with his band. Says he loves it and isn't sure when he'll be back. But I know my brother. He has his eye on a woman he met here at my grandfather's birthday party. He keeps asking about her, which is so unlike my brother. He'll be back."

"Sounds like you all are close."

"We are. Growing up, we were inseparable. Not to mention the host of cousins that lived here off and on, or spent summers and holidays here."

Bailey stared into her drink. "That's what I wanted," she said softly. "A close family that loved each other, supported each other, us against the world. You know." She took a sip, and her eyes fluttered closed for a moment.

He tossed her a smile. "Hey, do you swim?"

"I can manage in the water. Why?"

"Let's go for a moonlight swim."

She giggled. "Are you kidding?"

"Absolutely not."

"I don't have a bathing suit," she hedged.

He put his glass down, swung his long legs off the table and stood. "The water is always warm. No one here but us."

There was that smile again, and her heart started jumping.

Justin extended his hand. "Great way to relax," he continued to coax.

Bailey suddenly beamed a smile, took his hand and jumped up. "Let's go for it."

"Now you're talking."

They ran out back like two giddy high school kids who had the house to themselves while their parents were away.

"You sure no one can see us?" Bailey asked as she slowly began to strip.

Justin stepped out of his drawstring sweats. "If they could—" he voice grew thick as he looked at Bailey's lush body unveiled in front of him "—they would be very jealous that they could only see and not touch."

Her flesh heated from the lascivious look in his eyes.

"Woman, you could make a man lose his mind." He

stepped to her, reached around her back and unfastened her bra. He peeled it off and tossed it onto a lounge chair. He murmured something deep in his throat before letting his thumbs trail teasingly across the dark brown areolas. Bailey moaned softly. Justin lowered his head and took the right nipple into his mouth, let his tongue play and tease it until it was large and hard, and he could feel her body shiver against his. He hooked his fingers beneath the band of her panties and inched them down across her hips. She wiggled out of them.

Justin caressed her round hips and slid a finger inside her very moist slit. Her legs wobbled. She gripped his shoulders and rocked her pelvis against his hand. She then reached between them and took his hard phallus in her hand. Justin groaned as she stroked him, ran her thumb across the swollen head, and felt his dew dampen her fingertip.

He backed up to the lounge chair and sat. His hot gaze beckoned her. Bailey came to him, spread her legs on either side of the chair and slowly lowered herself on top of him. As always, that initial contact took their breaths away. For a moment, neither of them could move and then, slowly, Bailey began to ride him as he leaned back and took everything that she threw at him, returning the favor in kind.

Justin grabbed the globes of her rear and thrust up and deep. She cried out, and he pushed harder, holding her in place so that she was totally his for the taking. Bailey arched her back and thrust her hips forward, taking him even deeper inside.

"You're mine. All mine," he groaned between the valley of her breasts. "Mine," he repeated.

Bailey felt her world begin to shatter as the tingles raced up the backs of her legs, and her pulse roared in her ears. She threw her head back, and the moon and the stars looked down upon her as a volcanic orgasm snapped through her, shook her limbs, arrested her breath, clenched her walls to suck the essence of Justin out of him in an explosion that vibrated through the night.

She collapsed against his chest, and he held her. Their hearts banged and pounded as they tried to regain control over their breathing, that slowly turned to satiated laughter.

Justin kissed the hollow of her neck. "Woman…"

"Hmm…"

"I have no words."

"Hope that's a good thing."

"Trust me, it is." He cupped her face in his palms. His dark eyes skimmed her face. "I'm in love with you, Bailey."

She blinked rapidly.

"Don't say anything. I want that to sit with you for a while." He stroked her bottom lip with his thumb. "See how it fits."

"I don't have to see how it fits. I love you, too." She felt him pulse inside her.

"We'll make it work, babe."

She caressed his jaw. "I know." She slowly gyrated her hips against him.

Justin hissed between his teeth. "It's more than this," he groaned, thrusting up inside her. "Believe that."

She draped her arms around his neck and pressed her cheek against his. "I know," she whispered.

Chapter 19

"I need to go to Atlanta for a couple of days," Justin said while he prepared breakfast the following morning.

"Really? What's in Atlanta?"

"Hmm, just some business to handle."

"Okay. When are you leaving?"

"Tomorrow afternoon. I'll be back late Monday." He turned and spooned the omelet from the pan onto a platter.

Bailey looked at him. "Is everything okay?"

"Yeah, just some old business with a client that I need to tie up."

She bobbed her head and cut a slice of the omelet and put it on her plate. "I have to work Sunday anyway. We're hosting a private party."

Justin swung onto the stool. "No more issues with Vincent, I hope?"

"No. He's been cool. Distant but cool."

"Good. I know you were pissed that I said anything to him, but that's who I am. I can't sit around—" he leaned across the counter "—and have the woman I love disrespected. It's not gonna happen." He gave her a light peck on the lips.

Bailey's cheeks flamed. Love. Wow. This is what it feels like. A bubbling joy that could barely be contained. A warmth that flowed through your veins. A feeling that no matter what, that special someone was in your corner. She'd never had that. Never. It was hard to wrap her mind around the enormity of it, the responsibility of it. She'd felt love before, for her siblings, for Addy, but love had always been on the back burner when it came to her own life. Now, here it was. Right in front of her. This man loved her, and she was in love with him. A man who could have any woman he wanted. He chose her. Her.

"You okay? You're not eating," he said, breaking into her thoughts.

"Oh." She grinned. "Just thinking."

"About what?"

"About the fact that we never did get to swim last night."

Justin chuckled. "Yeah, I think we got a little distracted."

"Ya think!"

They both laughed.

"Listen, I know your car is still in the shop. What did they say about the repairs?"

Her expression drooped. "Hmm, the engine is shot."

"That's major."

"I know. Replacing the engine will cost more than the car is worth at this point."

Justin was thoughtful for a moment while he chewed his food. "Well, you can drive the Benz as long as you need to."

"I really can't do that. I can get a rental or something until…"

"Why do that when you have a car at your disposal?"

"Are you sure? You need your car."

"You need it more. And I have the Navigator." He didn't tell her that he also had other vehicles parked in the garage.

"If you're sure."

"Absolutely. Now eat up." He checked his watch. "I have some errands to run this morning."

"And I definitely need to get home and change, and check on Apryl."

"Speaking of home…I was thinking that since you'll

be spending more time here that you should bring some things over."

Her pulse quickened. "Bring some things over?"

Justin frowned and looked around the room. "Do you hear an echo?"

Bailey laughed. "Very funny. You sure?"

"Stop doubting what I say. Yes, I'm very sure."

She drew in a deep breath then grinned. "Okay. I will."

"Good. Then it's settled." He pushed back from the table and took his plate to the sink. "You think anymore about going with me to the foundation gala?"

"Not really. I've never been to anything like that before."

"And what was my promise to you?" he asked when he turned to face her. He rested against the sink.

She twisted her lips. "That you promise to take me to all the places I've wanted to go and have never been," she said softly.

"Exactly. So when you say the word, I'll make it happen."

He looked into her eyes, and she instantly knew that he understood the why of her reluctance.

She nodded her head in agreement. "Okay."

"Good. I'm going to grab a shower. You're welcome to join me." He gave her that tempting grin that made his eyes sparkle.

She got up from her seat and took her plate to the sink. "And we'd never get out of here." She lightly kissed his cheek that was slightly rough against her lips. "I think I like this rugged, after-five look on you." She caressed his jaw.

"Whatever makes you happy, babe." He lassoed his arms around her and pulled her close. "You like it, then I love it." He lowered his head and brushed his mouth against hers then slowly deepened the kiss, tasting the meal that they'd shared on her tongue, and he grew hungry again.

* * *

"I'm leaving for real this time," Bailey said over her laughter while Justin tried to entice her to stay in bed with him, where they'd eventually wound up. She scrambled out of bed as he tried to snatch her back. "And don't follow me," she said with a warning wag of her finger.

"I could make it worth your while."

"I'm sure you could." She gathered her clothes and went into the bathroom, shutting and locking the door behind her.

When she was dressed and ready to leave, she came out of the bathroom.

"I'll call you later," Justin said.

She reached up and gave him a quick kiss. "Okay. I go in tonight at six to set up for the private party. I'm off at one."

"Come here when you're done."

"Sounds inviting. I'll let you know. Okay?"

"Fair enough." He snatched her back before she crossed the threshold. "I love you."

Her pulse leaped. "I love you."

"Go, before I seriously change my mind about listening to you."

"Talk to you later." She spun away and practically skipped to the car. When she got behind the wheel of the Benz and looked at the expanse of the Lawson mansion in front of her and the man who loved her standing in the doorway, she felt as if she was in a dream, someone else's life. But it could be her life now, if she was willing to step into it. She turned the key in the ignition and slowly pulled out of the driveway. One day she was serving drinks behind those doors, and now she was sleeping with the man of the house.

When she arrived at her apartment, it seemed smaller than ever. She locked the door and put her purse on the kitchen table. She flipped through the mail that she'd taken

out of the mailbox on her way in. Bills, bills, overdue notices. There was one letter from Xavier University. Her
pulse quickened. She tore the envelope open. Her eyes
raced across the page. Her heart stopped. "We're sorry,
but at this time…" She didn't need to read any further.

She plopped down in the chair at the kitchen table. The
table rocked. What was she going to do now?

"Hi."

Bailey glanced over her shoulder. "Hi."

"Something wrong?"

"Nothing out of the ordinary." She stuck the letter back
in the envelope.

Apryl pulled out a chair and sat. "Sis, I'm really sorry
about the things I said. I was so out of line. You didn't
deserve that."

"How's your wrist?" she asked.

"Did you hear what I said?"

"I heard you."

"And? No response."

"What can I say, Apryl? You hurt me. Really hurt me
in a way I don't think you understand. I accept your apology, but that doesn't make the hurt go away. That's going
to take time." She glanced away. "How's your wrist?"

"Better. At least if you accept my apology, that's a
start."

Bailey offered her sister a shadow of a smile. "We all
have to start somewhere."

"I love you, sis."

Bailey's stomach jumped. Apryl had never said that to
her, not that way, not like she really meant it.

Apryl squeezed Bailey's hand. "Thanks for everything."
She pushed up from the table. "I think I'll go for a walk.
I need to get out of the house. I'll probably go home to-
morrow, give you your space back."

Bailey was speechless. Maybe her sister was growing
up after all.

* * *

Justin planned on using the family's Learjet. As long as someone else didn't need it, it should be available. If not, he'd book a quick round-trip flight to Atlanta. He put in a call to the hangar and spoke with the supervisor. Luckily, Desiree and her husband had just come back from Cancun that morning. After servicing and refueling, the supervisor told him it would be ready for Justin's trip to Atlanta. He'd have his usual pilot, Paul Harris. Although both Justin and Rafe had their pilot's license for a number of years, Justin preferred to relax this time. He had a lot to think about, and unwinding on the flight was exactly what he needed.

With that bit of business out of the way, Justin made a few phone calls, checked his email and was surprised to find one from Jasmine. She wanted to apologize for how she acted, the things she'd said. She missed him, and she hoped that they could find a way to fix things between them.

Justin pressed Delete, and the email zipped into the trash can. Next on his agenda was a trip into town to meet up with Dominique. His sister's keen eye for fashion was just what he needed. He knew what he liked to see on a woman, but Dominique knew what a woman wanted to be seen in.

Dominique was waiting for him in front of Femme Boutique. She'd assured him that something designer ready-to-wear could be found there.

"Hey, baby bro," she greeted.

"Hey yourself. Thanks for meeting me."

"Anything for you, sugah." She gave him a hug. "When am I going to get to meet this new lady of yours? Bailey, right?"

"Soon."

She hooked her arm through his. "Well, let's get this shopping party started."

Justin held the door open for her, and they walked inside.

"You can't go wrong with the little black dress," Dominique said, strutting through the aisle. She fingered a silk scarf as she passed. "I'm thinking cocktail length."

They were approached by a sales clerk. "How can I help you?"

"We're looking for a black cocktail dress, size ten. Flirty, but classy. Maybe something by Vera Wang."

"Right this way."

About an hour later, they were walking out with a dress that Justin couldn't wait to see Bailey in so that he could get her out of it."

"What about accessories?"

"Hmm, hadn't thought about that."

"Follow me over to my shop. I'm sure I can find the right thing."

Dominique had launched her business, First Impressions, nearly five years earlier. At first it was an outlet for the overflow of clothing that she'd acquired. Her idea was to provide a wardrobe jump start to women who were returning to the workforce, had hit on hard times or simply needed a designer outfit at rock-bottom prices. The business did so well, and her clientele was so devoted, that she expanded First Impressions to include GED classes and financial management courses. Both of which were always full with a waiting list. The expansion of her original building space was how she'd met her husband, Trevor—contractor extraordinaire. The one man on the planet that had been able to tame Dominique's wild ways—or at least rein her in a bit.

When they arrived at First Impressions, Dominique showed Justin the jewelry case that was lined with what looked like very expensive jewelry. She picked a rope choker coated in cubic zirconia that sparkled like diamonds, a real pair of diamond studs and a matching cuff bracelet. "On the house," she teased and put the items in a gift box.

"Thanks so much."

"I hope she appreciates you," Dominique said while she walked him to the door.

Justin stopped at the door. He looked at his sister. "I truly believe she does."

Justin kissed his sister's cheek. "Thanks for today, sis. Gotta go." He climbed into his Navigator and pulled off.

Chapter 20

Bailey picked through her closet and her dresser drawers and put a few items into a small carryall. A couple of tops, a pair of shorts, jeans, undies and lotion. The rest of her things were generally in her purse. She'd pick up a toothbrush and her favorite deodorant from the drugstore on her way to work.

She was still in a state of euphoria. She was in love, and the most incredible man was in love with her. Her sister, her flighty sister, finally admitted that she loved her. Bailey was in a good place in her soul. Better than she'd been in a long time—bills and no scholarship be damned. For now she was going to enjoy her time in the sun.

"Going away?" Apryl asked, appearing in the doorway of Bailey's room.

"No. Just putting a few things together to leave at Justin's place."

"Well, well. Sounds serious." She came into the room and sat on the side of Bailey's bed.

"Getting there," Bailey offered without saying more.

"I've left more of my *things* around town to fill a small boutique," she said in a self-deprecating way.

Bailey took a quick glance at her sister and was surprised to see the unhappiness that hung around the downturn of her mouth.

"One of these days I may get a drawer all my own." She looked up at her sister. "You're lucky. He really cares about you. I can tell. He'll make space for you in his closet and in his life." She snorted a laugh. "I know these things. My own love life may be shot to hell, but I can always predict someone else's."

Bailey sat down next to Apryl. "When you stop looking and when the time is right, the perfect man is going to walk right into your life. Stop chasing after love, sis."

Apryl rested her head on Bailey's shoulder the way she used to do when she was much younger. It still felt good. "I'll try to follow your advice."

Bailey arrived at the Mercury Lounge by six. The private party was scheduled to begin at eight. The third floor had been reserved, and the waitstaff was already setting up. They were expecting a party of seventy-five, some corporate bigwigs and their wives and guests. The party organizer had ordered top-shelf everything from the appetizers to the dessert.

Vincent was on his way down when Bailey arrived on the third level.

"Everything looks good," he said without preamble. "You can take it from here."

"Thanks."

He breezed by her without saying anything further. Bailey breathed a relieved sigh and entered the dining room. She reviewed the inventory and checked all of the carts. The third floor had its own kitchen for events like this, so she went to meet with the chef to ensure that he had everything he needed. With that last item out of the way, she met with the waitstaff supervisor for the event to go over the guest list and the staff for each table.

"I'll check in shortly. And you can reach me on the bluetooth if anything comes up throughout the night."

"Yes, Ms. Sinclair."

Bailey gave one last look around then went to the main level. She'd be doing double-duty tonight, but that was fine. It made the night go by faster.

On her first break of the evening, she called Justin to tell him to wait up for her, that she would come by when she got off work. He told her he was more than looking forward to it and would definitely make it worth the ride over.

With so much to look forward to, the night seemed to glide by. She felt good, deep-down-in-her-soul good. She went up to the third level to check on the guests and the service.

"Aren't you the one from the party?"

Bailey stopped short. She tilted her head in question. And then she recognized the woman in front of her. She was with Justin the night of the party, the one who made the catty remark about talking to the help.

"Good to see you again. Welcome to Mercury."

"What does he see in you?"

"You'd have to ask him."

"You'll never measure up," she said, stepping close. "He's intrigued for now. Something new. But he'll be back once he realizes that slumming isn't all it's cracked up to be."

"As long as you keep believing that. The real question is not what he sees in me but what did he ever see in you?"

Jasmine's eyes flared, and if looks could kill, someone would be preparing Bailey's eulogy. She took a sip from her glass of champagne and spun away.

Bailey was trembling inside. Fury spun in her gut like a tornado needing to let loose on someone or something. She conducted her work with professionalism even as she wanted to smack the smug look off Jasmine's face each time she fell into her line of sight. And every time, Jasmine would lean close to her conversation companion, giggle behind her hand and look in Bailey's direction.

Bailey went about her duties and instructed the staff before returning to the main level.

"What. Is. Wrong. With. You?" Mellie asked. "Who are you going to push out into traffic?"

Bailey wouldn't put the words together. To do so would give them more power than they were worth. Thinking about her brief run-in with Jasmine and her comments about Justin did leave her unsettled, though. How much truth was there in what Jasmine said? Hadn't she said the very same things herself? "Nothing," she finally said. "You know how the money folks can act."

"Hmm," she groused. "I know that's right. But at least they're good tippers."

"Yeah," Bailey said absently then walked down to the other end of the bar to serve a customer. *Just slumming.*

Bailey parked the car on the winding driveway of Justin's home. The lights on the ground floor were on. She could hear the faint sound of music coming from the house. This was the life that Jasmine claimed as hers, the life that Bailey only read about. Would Justin grow tired of her once he realized that she didn't fit in?

The front door opened, and Justin stood in the archway. He trotted down the steps and crossed the driveway to where Bailey was parked. She let the window down.

"Everything okay?" he asked, concern lacing his voice.

Bailey smiled. "Fine. Was just taking a minute."

"Rough night?"

"A little." She pressed the button to raise the window, shut off the car and got out.

Justin took her carryall, draped his arm around her shoulder then kissed the top of her head. "Let me see what I can do to make you feel better. I ran you a bath. Water's hot, wine is cold, and I've been known to give a mean massage."

She glanced up at him, and her spirit began to rise. "I like the sound of all of that."

"Right this way."

As promised, a hot bath was waiting, and the room held the aromatic scent of jasmine. The lights were dimmed, and candlelight flickered from the votives set strategically around the spa-size bath.

"Oh, Justin…" She turned to him and was greeted by his smile. Her heart swelled. "This is…" She was at a loss for words.

"This is all for you." He placed his hands on her shoulders. "Take as much time as you need. I'll bring you some wine. Want to hear some music while you unwind?"

"Sure," she whispered. "That would be wonderful."

"Your wish is my command." He crossed the heated mosaic tiles and pressed a button on a panel by the door. Soft, instrumental music floated through the air.

"Perfect."

Justin winked. "Be right back."

While he was gone, Bailey got undressed and stepped into the steamy water. Every muscle in her body moaned with pleasure as she slowly descended into the fragrant water. She leaned back against the headrest and closed her eyes, allowing the water to loosen her limbs.

"Here you go, babe."

Bailey's eyes fluttered open. Justin was sitting on the edge of the tub with a flute of wine in his hand.

She sighed with pleasure and took the glass. "Thank you."

"You can turn on the jets in the tub if you want."

"Thanks, I will."

He leaned over and kissed her lightly on the lips. "See you when you're done."

She nodded with a closemouthed smile.

Justin walked away and closed the door behind him. Bailey pressed the start button for the jets in the Jacuzzi, sipped her wine and experienced heaven.

She'd actually drifted to sleep, long enough that the hot water was now warm. She turned on the faucets and added more hot water, finished bathing and got out. A thick aqua-blue towel was laid out across a table. She dried off and wrapped herself in the towel that reached beyond her knees then opened the adjoining door that led to Justin's bedroom.

"Hey, feeling better?"

"Much."

"You can put whatever you want in the top two drawers and make whatever space you need in the closet if you have things you want to hang," he said from his seat by the window.

This was really happening. She was actually putting her clothing in Justin's home. He'd made space for her. This was no simple act; this was taking their relationship to another level.

"You're sure about this?"

He glanced up from what he was doing on his laptop. "Sure about what, babe?"

She felt silly asking, but she needed to hear the words. "Sure about me…taking up space."

Justin closed the cover of his laptop, set it on the table next to him and got up. He crossed over to where she was standing. He placed his hands on her shoulders and gazed down into her eyes. "Listen, you can take up all the space you want with me, in my home and in my life. Okay?"

Bailey blinked back the sudden burn in her eyes. "Okay."

"And don't you think for one minute that you don't belong here. You do. You belong here because I want you to be here." He stepped closer and put his arms around her waist. "Now that we have that out of the way, you hungry or do you want to turn in?"

"I'm really tired. I think I'll turn in."

"Cool. I have a few cases to review. As soon as I'm done, I'll give you that massage that I promised."

Bailey grinned. "Looking forward to experiencing your skills."

"Oh, baby, you have experienced my skills." He winked and walked back to his seat by the window.

While Justin worked, Bailey unpacked her carryall, putting undies and some tops in the drawer and her toiletries in the bathroom. She had brought two pairs of jeans and blouses for work that she hung in the deep walk-in closet. He had enough designer clothes and shoes to start a small boutique. She added her meager belongings.

"There's a box on the bottom shelf. It's for you," Justin called out.

Bailey looked at the sleek black box with the gold embossed letters of Femme Boutique. Her heart pounded. She gingerly lifted the box and brought it out of the closet. She placed it on the bed.

"Go ahead. Open it. I swear it won't bite."

"Justin…"

"Open it."

She lifted the cover, and her breath caught when she lifted back the scented tissue paper. Tucked in the box was a black dress that seemed to glisten from the hand-sewn insets across the bodice. She tenderly lifted the dress and held it up. It was a dress straight out of one of the top fashion magazines. The bodice was sleeveless and fitted, sprinkled with stones that looked like diamonds. The top was heart-shaped and tapered down to a flounced skirt of silk and tulle, that was both sexy and flirty.

Bailey held the dress up to her body and imagined herself in it. "Oh, Justin…it's beautiful." She spun toward him and was rewarded with his devastating smile.

"There's more."

"More?" She whirled back to the box, and beneath the tissue paper was two boxes from First Impressions. She opened the long box that held the bracelet and choker. She couldn't believe her eyes. Then she opened the smaller box and a pair of diamond earrings twinkled back at her. "Oh, my God. I don't believe this."

"Can't wait to see you in it."

"Justin…this is too much."

"Naw. I thought it would be a good incentive for you to get all dressed up and come with me to the foundation gala. And I wanted to do something special for you."

She clung to the dress as if she couldn't believe it was real. "You've done so much already."

Justin crossed his right ankle over his left knee and leaned forward. "Babe, anything I do for you is because I want to."

"But I can't do anything for you…nothing like this."

"This isn't tit for tat. I'm not looking for anything. What you can do for me is be happy and let me be there for you." He got up and came to her. He took the dress from her hands and put it on the bed. "Let me love you, Bailey."

Her body flooded with heat. That was the second time he'd uttered the word *love*. Was it simply an endearing phrase that he used, or did it have real meaning? Did he love her? Really love her?

"Love me?" she murmured.

"Yes, love you. And I don't mean *make* love to you. I mean love you, the way a man loves a woman, the way I want to love you, totally and without reservation." He paused and searched her open expression. "Let me." He didn't give her time or room to respond. He covered her mouth with his and reconfirmed his declaration.

She melted against him, sank into the essence of him, absorbed him through her pores and when her towel fell away and tumbled at her feet, she loved him back with every ounce of her being.

Chapter 21

Justin pulled up in his driveway just as twilight was beginning to settle, that in-between time when it's hard to determine fact from fiction. But whatever doubts and feelings of uncertainty he'd been having today about his career path were erased when he spotted the Benz already parked. His wavering spirits soared.

Bailey was curled up on the couch intently watching the new Omari Hardwick series when Justin walked in. She hopped to her feet, and he pulled her into his arms. She'd never felt so good to him as she did now. He held her close, kissed her cheeks, her ears, her lips as if he had to assure himself that she was really here. That this was real.

"You don't know how much this means having you here now, today," he breathed into her hair.

She stepped back, looked up at him and cupped his face in her palms. Her eyes scored his taut expression. "What is it? What's wrong?"

He looked away and released her then walked over to the bar and poured a quick glass of bourbon. "You want something?"

"Do I need something?"

He tossed the drink down his throat, savored the warmth then set the glass down. He leaned back against the bar, folded his arms. Bailey sensed that she needed to sit down and she did.

"I had a conversation with my father today. He is tying himself in knots about me leaving the firm to launch The

Justice Project. He went on and on about how I was going to ruin my legal career, mess up my connections to some of the most influential people in Baton Rouge." He shook his head with annoyance. "I told him in no uncertain terms that it was long past the time when he could dictate my life to me. He was either going to support me, or...walk away." He took a swallow of his drink. "He then said he had an 'important call coming in.' and had to go." He snorted a laugh then shrugged. "Branford Lawson isn't used to his way not being 'the' way."

She pushed up from her seat and walked up to him. She took his hands. "I'm here. We're in this together, whatever way it works out."

Relief softened the lines around his eyes. A smile of thanks lifted his mouth. "This is why I love you," he whispered, before covering her lips with his.

They spent the rest of the evening talking about what the future would hold for both of them—Justin's pursuing his new venture and her returning to law school.

"So have you heard anything yet from the schools that you applied to?"

She shook her head. "I can pretty much go wherever I want *if* I had the money to pay for it." She snorted a laugh. "I've gotten a couple of partial scholarships but nowhere near what I need. But I'm hopeful. I'm still waiting on the big one—Harvard. They're really trying to elevate their diversity, and they have money."

"Harvard... You'd have to leave..."

She stole a glance at him and nodded slowly. "But I still haven't heard anything. The letters should be going out soon."

"I can help you."

"Help me? What do you mean?"

"I can pay for your classes."

"Are you kidding me? No. I don't want you to do that, and I didn't tell you about it because I wanted a handout!"

He levered up on his elbow and clasped her bare shoulder. "It's not a handout, Bailey. Why is it so hard for you to accept anything from me? I'm not like those other men, and you're not your mother."

She swung her head away. It was a constant war that she waged within herself. More so now than ever before in her life. She could easily see herself falling headlong into all the trappings that came with a life that Justin could offer. First the car, then space in his closet, then keys to his door, the dress, jewelry and now he was offering to help pay her tuition. What next? How much of her independence was she willing to lose?

"I can't let you do that," she said softly. "This is my dream—just like you have yours. I need to do this for me. And if I can't, then I guess it wasn't meant to be."

"I moved some stuff into Justin's house," Bailey said as she sorted through her mail.

"Wow. So now what?"

"Now we…" Her heart thumped. "Addy…its a letter from Harvard." Her fingers trembled.

Addison jumped up from the couch. "Open it!"

"I'm scared. What if I don't get in?"

"But what if you do? Open it."

Bailey drew in a breath and stuck her thumb under the flap of the envelope and peeled it open. Slowly she unfolded the letter. Her eyes raced across the words. "Oh, my God, oh, my God!" She squeezed the letter to her chest.

"What? What?"

"I got a full-year scholarship to freaking Harvard!" She jumped up and down and spun in a circle of joy.

Addison started screaming, too, as if she'd won the lottery and then wrapped Bailey in a hug. "I'm so happy for you. Everything is coming together for you. Finally. And you deserve it, girl. You deserve it."

Tears pooled in Bailey's eyes. "Thank you," she sniffed

and then read the letter again through her misty eyes. "This is so incredible." She sat at the wobbly kitchen table and stared at the letter—at her future.

"So...when would you have to leave?"

Leave. The word rocked her inside. That was the reality. She would have to leave. Leave her family, her life here—Justin.

"Classes start in five weeks," she said softly.

"How do you think Justin will take it?"

"I don't know."

"I'm sure the two of you will work it out. He wants you to have your dream as much as you do. Long-distance relationships can work if the couples are willing and committed to it. Besides, your man has the means to see you whenever you want."

"Yes," she said almost to herself. "He certainly does."

Chapter 22

Bailey stared at her reflection in the full-length mirror. The dress fit as if it had been made especially for her. The garment hugged her upper body, showcasing her narrow waist and full breasts that teased above the heart-shaped dip of the bodice. From the waist the silk-and-tulle skirt floated out and around her knees. Her jewelry sparkled, and for the first time in her life she felt like she was living the fairy tale of her dress.

"Oh, baby…" Justin murmured in deep appreciation.

She turned from the mirror and gave him the full effect but was hit by a jolt of lightning when she laid eyes on him.

The cut of his tuxedo accentuated his broad shoulders and washboard abs. He opted to go tie-less, which gave him an elegant yet cavalier appearance, and the slight shadow around his jaw only added another level of delicious sexiness.

Bailey beamed then gave him a little twirl before dancing over to him. He looped his arm around her waist and gently swayed with her. "You'll be the most beautiful belle at the ball," he said then lowered her into a dip that had her giggling with happiness.

"Exactly how many cars do you have?" Bailey asked, wide-eyed when Justin opened her door to the Lexus.

He gave an indifferent shrug. "A couple." He shut her door and came around to the driver's side and got in.

"How many is a couple?"

He turned the key, and the car purred to life. The lush leather seating enveloped her, and she felt as if she was being held in the palm of a hand. The dash gleamed with lights and buttons and the sound system was to die for.

"The Benz, the Navigator, the Jaguar, this…and a Mustang convertible," he added.

Bailey shook her head in amazement. What could one person need with so many cars? But the reality was, if he didn't have more than one car, she would have been in debt with a rental, since she'd told the mechanic to junk the car.

"I have a confession to make," Bailey said.

"What?"

"I'm sure you must have guessed it, but I've never been to one of these things before, at least not as a guest."

"No big deal, really. Just a lot of people who got all dressed up to drink and gossip and spend money—for a worthy cause. It'll be fine. And as soon as I make the rounds, shake a few hands, we can leave if you want. Deal?"

"Deal." She relaxed against the headrest.

Justin drove with his left hand and placed his right hand on her thigh. A shiver fluttered up her leg.

"I'm going to be shaking hands really quickly," he said, his voice having grown thick, as his fingers stroked her inner thigh.

Bailey's lids drifted closed. She covered his hand with hers to stop his trip up her skirt. "We'll never get there and get back if you keep that up."

Justin snatched a look at her. "Yeah, real fast handshakes."

The foundation gala was being held at the Ritz Carlton Hotel, and the decked and bejeweled guests were out in force. Bailey felt as if she'd stepped into the pre-Oscar show hour as she and Justin walked arm in arm down the length of the red carpet and up the marble stairs to the entrance. The annual foundation gala for cancer research brought out the media, who took as many pictures as possible as the well-heeled guests arrived, calling out to them, asking who they were with and what the women were wearing.

Bailey was overwhelmed and held on tight to Justin, who seemed to be less than interested in the hoopla or maybe it was the fact that he was so accustomed to these things that it no longer fazed him.

Once inside, they were directed to the main ballroom, which was something right out of a magazine. Crystal chandeliers splashed diamond-like light across the expanse of the room that was dotted with large circular tables—to seat ten—all topped with bursts of flowers in tall glasses, gleaming silverware and hand-designed china. Waiters floated around with trays of champagne.

Justin reached in his pocket and pulled out the invitation. "We're up front. Table three." He stuck the invitation back into his pocket before stopping a waiter. He took two glasses of champagne from the tray and handed one to Bailey. "May this part of the evening fly by," he said with a wink and tipped his glass to hers.

Bailey's teasing glance caught him over the rim of her glass. "Let the handshaking begin."

They settled themselves at their table after Justin ran into several of the guests that he knew, and each time he proudly introduced Bailey as "my lovely lady." She couldn't remember ever having been claimed like that by a man in public. It made her feel valued in a way that she hadn't experienced before. And he didn't say the things he did, or do the things he did for her because he could get something out of it. She had nothing to offer but herself. And that seemed to be enough for him, which made keeping the news from him about the letter from Harvard that much more difficult. She knew she couldn't wait much longer.

Shortly after they were seated, Carl and his wife, Gina, arrived, and Gina and Bailey hit it right off. Before long they were talking like old friends that had plenty in common. Bailey wanted Gina to meet Addison, and they talked about setting up a girls' night.

The entrées were served, and the formal part of the evening was under way. The waiters were taking away the plates and preparing to serve the next course when Jasmine appeared at the table with her cousin Stephanie.

"Justin. Hello."

"Jasmine."

Her light brown eyes roamed the table, acknowledged Carl and Gina then settled on Bailey. "I wouldn't expect to see you here."

"And why would that be?" Bailey tossed back.

Jasmine gave a shrug. "I mean, I didn't think that you could get time off from bartending."

Stephanie snickered.

Justin rose, towering over her. He got close, lowered his voice to a stern whisper. "I'm going to tell you this for the last time. We're done. We will never be. Bailey is with me. You don't have to like it. I don't give a damn. But you will respect her."

The color beneath her cheeks heightened. Her nostrils flared as if she couldn't breathe as she blinked back the sting in her eyes.

Stephanie took her arm. "Come on. There's nothing going on over here."

Jasmine looked at Justin with a defeated pain in her eyes before she turned and followed her cousin.

Justin's chest heaved. He sat down, his face stoney. Bailey covered his clenched fist. "Thank you," she mouthed. He leaned over and kissed her lightly.

"Now that we've got that bitch, I mean, business, out of the way, let's eat," Gina said, breaking the last lock of tension at the table.

* * *

As promised, once the meal was over, Justin and Bailey began inching their way to the exit before all the long-winded speeches and awards were presented. He'd already made his five-thousand-dollar contribution, so there was nothing keeping him there, and he was eager to get Bailey out of that dress that had been driving him crazy all night.

This time she didn't stop him when his fingers roamed higher and higher up her skirt to tease the thin covering over her crotch. She could feel herself growing slick with need as she pressed her hand over his to cup it in place. It had taken twenty minutes to get to the hotel, but it seemed to take an eternity to get home.

"I think you'd better take that off. If I get my hands on it I may rip up a perfectly beautiful dress."

"With pleasure," she cooed and blew him a kiss before giving him her back to undo her zipper. "And for now, be gentle."

He made slow work of unzipping her, kissing each inch of succulent flesh as it exposed itself to his hungry eyes.

Bailey quivered as the heat of his kisses shimmied up and down her spine. He peeled the dress away, and she stepped out of it. Justin turned her around; her bare, full breasts brushed against his tux jacket and lit her nipples afire.

"Damn," he groaned before embarking on the feast of her offerings. He lifted the weight of her breasts in his palms and guided them to his mouth. His tongue teased each nipple, nibbling and laving them until they were hard, dark pebbles.

Bailey's fingertips dug into the hard knots of muscle in his arms while she arched her back to give him better access.

"I want to take you, right here, just like this," he said, his breath a hot hiss against her skin. He hooked his fingers along the elastic of her black panties and tugged them down, slid two fingers inside her that took her breath away.

She kicked her panties away and pulled his jacket from his body. The buttons of his shirt were determined to stay in place, but she was just as determined. With his shirt finally undone, the hard span of his chest was hers for the taking, and she took. Her tongue danced along his skin, suckled his nipples, teased the hard lines of his arms while she unfastened his buckle and unzipped him. She took him in her palm and felt him pulse along with the almost painful moan that left his lips. Bailey lowered herself, bit by bit until the head of his cock brushed her lips. She flicked her tongue along the dewy head and was rewarded with his outcry of her name. Little by little she took him in, sucking and licking until he filled the cavern of her mouth to the back of her throat. She wanted all of him, but she'd taken in all that she could. She stroked the rest until he began to rock his pelvis against her mouth. His fingers dug into her hair.

"Ahhh, babe…" He sucked in air through his teeth. He grabbed either side of her head. "Gotta…stop," he managed, even as he continued to thrust against her willing mouth. Then he pulled out and stumbled back, breathing heavily. His eyes were blazing dark pools as if an oil field had been set on fire.

Bailey's wet, puffy lips parted as she looked up at him with her own kind of hunger. He pulled her to her feet and unceremoniously scooped her up and carried her up to his bedroom.

When Justin entered her, she exploded. The sudden intensity of her orgasm slammed through her like an electric charge. Her body vibrated, and she cried out. The pitch of her joy hung in the torrid air. Justin wasn't ready to let go yet. He wanted to remain buried inside her heat and held captive between her thighs.

Bailey moaned and rotated her hips as Justin continued to move within her as her own release began to ebb, then by degrees rise to meet the thrill that Justin stirred inside her. She felt that she would burst from his fullness while his ride toward release intensified with every thrust that became faster, deeper, harder. His breathing escalated, a sheen of sweat dampening his skin. His groans grew heavier. She tightened her hold on him.

"Come. Come to me," she whispered deep in his ear.

The erotic words mixed with the quick sucking of her insides on his throbbing member sent him hurtling over the edge.

"That was…there are no words," Bailey said.

"My sentiments exactly." He kissed the back of her neck and pulled her closer. He sighed in satisfaction. "It's good having you here." He kissed her again.

"I like being here."

"There's plenty more room in the closets," he said suggestively.

For an instant, she froze. "What are you saying?"

"I'm saying that I have no problem with you being here…full-time."

She turned over. Her eyes searched his face in the dimness. "Move in?"

"Why not? Plenty of space."

She paused. "Justin, I need to tell you something." She felt him tense.

"What is it?"

"I got the letter from Harvard. They offered me a scholarship for a year, and…I'm going to take it."

The seconds of silence were eternal.

"Babe, that's amazing. I'm so happy for you. I know how much you want this." He gathered her close, bringing her into the hollow of his neck. He stared out into the darkness. "Harvard. That is big-time. When would you have to leave?"

"Umm, five weeks. I have to look for off-campus housing." She fluttered a laugh. "I think I'm a bit old to live in a dorm."

Justin chuckled absently. "Very true…not saying that you're old or anything," he added in jest.

Bailey nudged him. She drew in a breath. "I know this is going to change things between us…the distance. But I want us to find a way to work it out." She clutched his shoulder and tried to gauge his expression.

He kissed the top of her head. "Of course we will. Let's not worry about that now. You have plans to make."

Chapter 23

"Harvard. That's major," Carl said. He lifted his bottle of Coors and took a long swallow. "How is that going to play out with you two?"

Justin stretched out on the lounge chair on the back deck, tucked his hands beneath his head and closed his eyes against the setting sun. A light evening breeze ruffled the trees.

"Good question. We were just settling into a rhythm. I gave her a key."

"You what?"

"Yeah, man."

"That's a serious move."

"That's how I'm feeling about her—serious."

"Man. Well, they say that long-distance relationships can work," he said without much conviction.

"They who?"

"You know. Them. Those people that take those surveys."

"And you would know that how?"

"I hear things."

Justin cut him a look. "Whatever, man." He paused. "Would you do it?"

"Have a long-distance relationship?"

"Yes."

"I guess it depends on how long and how invested I was."

"What if it was Gina?"

"Hmm. If you'd asked me that before we got married, I probably would have said no. Now…it would be hard, but I'd do it if it would keep us together. I can't see myself without Gina."

Justin sighed heavily. Maintaining a relationship was tough enough with all the curves that life could throw, then add in long distance and you were asking for trouble.

"What about Xavier or LSU?" Carl asked, cutting into Justin's thoughts.

"She's going on scholarship."

Carl's brows rose then fell. "Oh."

"Oh, what?"

"Nothing. I'm just saying, oh." He waited a beat. "If it's about money…maybe you could help her out and then she could stay."

"Ha! You don't know Bailey. She's so damned independent and determined to do everything on her own, her way, that she'd cut my head off for even suggesting it. I hinted at it once before and she went nuclear. Naw, not an option."

"Then you don't have much of a choice. She's going to Harvard, and you are either going the long-distance route or walking away."

Justin closed his eyes. Walking away wasn't in the plan.

Bailey hurried through the main level of the Mercury Lounge and went straight to her office. Since the one-on-one between Vincent and Justin, Vincent had remained on the perimeter of her life. They only spoke about business, and to be honest, she missed their former camaraderie— at least what she thought was a friendship. Soon it would all be moot anyway. She had to give her notice, and she needed to do that sooner rather than later.

She stowed her purse in her desk drawer, locked it then turned on the computer to verify the staffing for the night. With that out of the way, she wanted to have the conversation with Vincent and get that out of the way, too. She didn't want the knowledge of her departure and the ensuing conversation to hang over her head longer than necessary.

Bailey stepped out of her office, locked the door and then walked farther down the hall to Vincent's office. She hoped he was there and that she wouldn't have to make a "special time" to talk to him.

A stream of light peeked out from under his door. She moved forward. Stopping in front, she drew in a breath of resolve and knocked on the door.

"Come in."

Bailey opened the door and stepped in. "Vincent, I want to talk to you."

"What is it?" he asked without looking up.

Bailey stepped closer and sat down in the chair by his desk. "You know that my long-term goal was to go back to law school."

He glanced up at her through his lashes then looked back at what he was writing. "And?"

"Well, I got accepted to Harvard. Classes start in five weeks. I'm giving my two-weeks' notice."

Vincent put down his pen, pushed back and leaned in his seat and looked at her. "Congratulations. I know that's what you wanted."

"Yes, it is." She dared to smile, being hard-pressed to contain her excitement.

He was thoughtful for a moment, and his steady stare was making Bailey uncomfortable.

"You're going to be hard to replace. But there comes a time when we all have to move on to bigger and better things. Good luck."

"Thank you, Vincent. And thank you for giving me a chance here." She pushed up from her seat and stood. "I better get to my station."

"No need."

"Huh?"

"You can leave tonight. No reason to drag out the inevitable."

Her mouth dropped open. "But I still have three weeks to work," she cried.

He gave a slight shrug. "We'll mail you your check."

She was so furious that she could barely see in front of her. He was really going to screw her like this? Her entire body was white-hot with rage, but she'd never let him see her sweat. "Fine. I'll get my things and be gone." Her throat tightened. She spun away and walked out.

When she unlocked the door to her office her hands were shaking, and tears of fury and impotence stung her eyes. Was he really that vindictive? What was she going to do for money? She had bills to pay and plans to make. Damn you, Vincent!

Through blurry eyes, she went through her desk and took out any personal items, which were few. She put her files on a flash drive that she kept in her purse, took a last look around and walked out.

When she arrived at what would have been her post for the night, Mellie instantly knew that something was wrong.

"What's going on? Are you all right?"

Bailey blinked away the sting of her tears. She took her office keys out of her purse and placed them on the bar top. "I no longer work here."

"What!"

Bailey gave her the abbreviated version.

"I'm happy for you, Bailey. I know how much you wanted it. This is your shot, girl, but I'm going to miss you like crazy." She shook her head slowly. "I can't believe that bastard did that to you."

"I can't worry about it."

"Are you going to be okay money-wise?"

"I'll work it out."

Mellie reached across the bar and covered her hand. "Stay in touch, okay?"

"I will. Promise." She offered a tight smile, turned and walked out. By the time she walked the half block to where she'd parked, the tears were flowing in earnest. A wave of panic assaulted her. What was she going to do? Five weeks without an income?

She'd told Justin earlier that she would come to his house when she got off, but she wasn't up to seeing him. She couldn't have him know how bad things were and how scared she was. But he'd be expecting her. She'd call him when she got home.

When she got home, all she had the will to do was stretch out on her bed and stare at the ceiling. She had to figure something out, but her thoughts kept swimming in endless circles. At some point she must have dozed off, and it was the ringing of her cell phone that jerked her out of a restless sleep.

She fumbled with the phone in the dark. Justin.

"Hey," she said, trying to sound cheery and wide-awake.

"Hey yourself. How's everything going? You sounded like you were sleeping." He chuckled.

"I...was actually."

"Sleeping on the job?"

"I'm home."

"Are you sick? What's wrong?"

"Silly me, I got my schedule wrong. I wasn't on for tonight."

Justin let the silence hang there for a minute. "What happened, Bailey? As organized and precise as you are, that would never happen."

"Can we talk tomorrow? I'm really tired."

"You're not going to tell me what's wrong?"

"Nothing. Nothing that I can't handle with a little sleep."

"This isn't cool. I'm not going to ask you anymore. But know that this isn't cool. Whatever is going on with you, we are in it together. But we can't be if you want to keep walking the line by yourself when you don't have to."

"Vincent let me go tonight."

"Say what?"

She squeezed her eyes shut and visualized the steely look that she was certain was on Justin's face. "I told him that I would be leaving in five weeks for school and I was giving my two-weeks' notice. He basically told me there was no reason to finish out my two weeks and that tonight was my last day."

He muttered an expletive. "I'm coming over. Answer the door."

"Justin!"

He'd already hung up.

Bailey got up from the bed and began pacing her apartment. Justin was right; she should feel comfortable enough to tell him anything, and not be leery of asking for advice or help or support. But old habits die hard. She was constantly battling the demons of her past. Already she could see herself falling into the trap of being taken care of by a man. The car. The dress. His coming to her defense the first time with Vincent. The key to his house. All of those were small things when looked at singularly. But together they added up to becoming dependent on someone else for your survival, for your happiness. She couldn't do it. Even though he'd said he loved her, it was still hard to let go.

More than an hour had passed since she'd spoken to Justin. It didn't take that long to get from his part of town to hers. She hoped nothing had happened and went to the window to see if his car was coming, just as her downstairs doorbell rang. She buzzed him in.

When she pulled open the door and saw him standing there with nothing but love in his eyes, her soul opened up, and she fell into his arms. She inhaled him like fuel for an engine and he held her, not saying a word. He didn't need to, because she realized that his being there said everything.

"Come in," she finally said when she could let him go.

Justin closed the door behind him. "Apryl here?"

"She went back home. She said she wanted to give me back my space. Can I get you anything?"

"No. I'm good." He sat on the couch and extended his hand to her. She took it and sat beside him. He draped his arm around her shoulder. "First of all, if that's the way he wants to treat you after the time and service that you put in to make his establishment successful, the hell with him. It's his loss. And it shows you the kind of man he really is." He reached in his pocket and pulled out an envelope. "After our little chat, he seemed to understand the error of his way of thinking." He handed her the envelope.

"What is this?"

"Open it and see for yourself."

Hesitantly she took the envelope and opened it. Inside was a check for easily twice the amount that she was owed. She stared at the numbers in disbelief then turned wide eyes on Justin.

"What is this? How...?"

"He owed it. He paid it."

"Justin. What did you do?"

"I didn't break his knees, if that's what you're thinking," he said in jest. "I simply had a talk with him. When I finished talking, he understood how wrong he was and wanted to make it up to you."

She studied his expression, which didn't change from its matter-of-fact demeanor, as if convincing people to do what he wanted, to buy into his idea, was second nature. The truth—it was. He was a seasoned attorney who molded, spun and presented information for a living—a good living. She had no idea what she was going to do being out of a job and with no money in sight. Now, thanks to Justin, it was a non-issue. Then she felt that old demon slip in under the door and take a seat in between them. This was all part of the same pattern of turning yourself over to someone else; giving them the power over you and the direction your life would take. It was easy to succumb when your back was against a wall, easy to simply "let it happen," because there was no other way, until one day you didn't know who you were, and when your almighty benefactor left, you were left with nothing and no one.

Bailey stared at the check. Her thoughts twisted in her head. "Thank you," she said finally.

"You take what is owed to you. All the time. Every time. If you are going to be a lawyer, that's one of the first lessons of making a deal. You must make your opponent believe that negotiating is to their benefit, when in the end, its yours." He leaned over and kissed her forehead.

"I'll try to remember that."

"Speaking of becoming a lawyer, what are you going to do about someplace to live?"

"The school mailed a list of off-campus housing. I'm going to make a few calls. Now that I have time on my hands…"

"How do you see things working out between you and me?"

She sighed heavily. "To be honest, I don't know." She turned her body toward his. "I want us to work. I need us to work. Whatever it takes. I know it won't be easy."

"And with me working to get The Justice Project up and running, it will put us to the test." He stroked her face. "I always did well on tests," he said, his voice dropping an octave.

Bailey grinned. "So did I. Top of my class."

He leaned in. "Impressive," he uttered before melding his lips with hers. "Me, too."

Chapter 24

"Girl, not only is the man wealthy and sexy as hell, he's a damn superhero, too."

Bailey burst out laughing. "Addy, you are a pure fool."

"What else do you call a man who 'comes to the rescue?' He's been there for you from the start. You are one lucky woman."

"I know that I should feel lucky. I know that I am."

"But?"

"But I feel that the more he gives, the more he offers, the more I will lose of myself."

"Do you know how many women would love to be in your shoes?"

"Hmm." She continued cutting up the cucumbers for the salad. Addison had a bridal shower that she was catering for, and since Bailey had the time, she offered to help with the preparations.

"I'm going to miss you when you leave."

Bailey began to rinse and devein the shrimp. "I'm going to miss you like crazy," she said just above a tight whisper. "But we can visit, write. I'll try to come down on breaks…"

"But it won't be the same." Addison sighed.

"I know," Bailey said as she tossed the shrimp shells onto a layer of newspaper.

As much as she tried to pretend that life would remain virtually unchanged, she knew she was deluding herself. But this was her chance. She had to take it or she would never forgive herself, even if taking that chance meant leaving the ones you love behind.

During the next few weeks leading up to her departure, she realized day by day what a blessing in disguise it was to be let go early from the Mercury Lounge. Every day there was an endless list of things to do. She'd finally decided on a one-bedroom apartment, about six blocks from campus. She'd taken a virtual tour, spoke with the landlord and then mailed her month's rent and security. The next step was packing and having her belongings shipped up. Fortunately, her current lease was month to month, and she'd given her current landlord plenty of notice.

Bailey came back from The Home Depot with more boxes. She stopped at her mailbox and checked for mail while also making a mental note to stop by the post office and have her mail forwarded.

Her sisters were already in her apartment to help with the packing when she returned. Seeing them together, laughing and teasing each other, filled her soul with a kind of joy that was hard to name.

"Hey, folks," she announced, dropping the boxes by the door and tossing the mail on the table. She stood in the center of the chaos with her hands on her hips, taking it all in.

"I sorted all the clothes," Tory said. "By season. Your warmer things are marked. You'll need those first."

"Your books are all boxed up, and I just finished up with your pots and dishes. I left a couple out for you to use until…you leave," Apryl said.

"You guys are so wonderful. I'm practically packed." Bailey grinned.

"We wanted to do this. You're forever putting your life on hold for us, sacrificing for us. It's way past time that we took care of ourselves and let you have a life, go after your own happiness," Apryl said.

Bailey could barely believe the words she was hearing. She'd longed for them, but never thought she'd hear them. "Thank you," she choked.

"That doesn't mean that I'm not still going to be a pain in the ass," Tory teased.

Apryl threw a pillow from the couch at Tory and they all laughed and hugged and laughed some more.

When her sisters had piled out of her tiny apartment, she looked around at the stack of boxes and the empty cabinets. A chapter of her life was closing, and a new one would begin very soon.

So much had happened in the past few months. If anyone would have told her that she would have found the love of an amazing man, got admitted into one of the top law schools in the country, would be leaving her home state of Louisiana and had forged a new and mature relationship with her sisters, she wouldn't have believed it. Life.

She stepped around the boxes stacked neatly in her living room, picked up her mail from the kitchen table and took it to her bedroom. She tossed it on the nightstand, and the familiar Louisiana State University logo, sticking out from a magazine, stopped her cold. She lifted up the magazine and plucked out the letter that had been stuck in between the pages. She flipped the envelope over and ripped open the flap. Her heart raced as she read the letter of congratulations. The letter stated that she was being considered for a full scholarship at LSU for the fall, and the admissions committee wanted to arrange an interview on August 10. Tomorrow!

Bailey spun around in a circle of crazy excitement. She read the letter three times to make sure that she had not misread it. She didn't. They wanted to meet with her.

She tucked the letter back into the envelope, picked up her cell phone and called Justin. She was so giddy with excitement, he had to ask her to slow down and repeat herself.

"Babe, that is incredible. Talk about the eleventh hour. What time tomorrow?"

"Noon."

"Okay. I was going to tell you to come over, but you need a good night's sleep so that you will be at the top of your game tomorrow. But I know you are going to wow them. It's probably all formality. It's yours. I just know it."

"Oh, Justin. This would mean I could stay here."

"It would. Are you willing to let go of the idea of Harvard?"

She was quiet for a moment. "I would still get to attend law school and I would be here with you."

"I want you to be happy."

"I am, Justin, happier than I have been in a very long time, and I owe so much of that happiness to you."

"I love you, Bailey. Whatever it takes to show you…"

"The way you love me…"

"What, babe? The way I love you, what?"

"Makes me feel…like someone who'd been dying of thirst and that thirst is finally quenched. I feel whole, valued."

"And for as long as you let me, I'm going to do everything in my power to keep you feeling that way. Now, you get some rest. Call me in the morning."

"Okay. I will."

"Good night."

"I love you," she said softly.

"And I love to hear you say it. Now, go to bed. Dream of tomorrow and us."

She grinned from the inside out. "Night."

Bailey had taken extra time preparing for her interview. She'd gone over and over in her head the kinds of questions that might be tossed at her so that she could be ready for any eventuality. She arrived with more than twenty minutes to spare before her scheduled appointment. She cooled her heels in the reception waiting area and bided her time watching the comings and goings of staff. Finally, the assistant to the dean of admissions came over and said to follow her.

She was led down a long, carpeted corridor, whose walls were dotted with large framed photographs of the learned and somber faces of past college presidents and chairmen. It was a bit intimidating, but Bailey took it in stride. She deserved to be here.

The assistant opened a heavy mahogany door and stepped aside so that Bailey could enter.

"Dean Withers, this is Ms. Sinclair."

Coleman Withers removed his half-frame glasses and smiled up at Bailey. He rose from his seat and came around his desk. "Ms. Sinclair." He extended his hand, which she shook. "Thank you for coming."

"I should be thanking you."

"Please have a seat. Can I get you anything?"

"Water would be fine."

He looked to his assistant. "Would you bring us some water, Diane?"

"Right away."

"Have any trouble finding us?" he mildly joked.

Bailey smiled. "No, not at all. Parking is a bit of a maze."

He chuckled. "Yes, it's been the battle cry for years, but—" he gave a slight shrug "—we've accepted it as part of the LSU charm."

Whatever anxiety that Bailey had been feeling peeled away. Dean Withers made her feel totally comfortable and relaxed.

His assistant returned with a glass pitcher of water and glasses on a tray. She set them on the table. "Will you be needing anything else?"

"No. Thank you, Diane.

"So, tell me about yourself and why you want to come to LSU."

Bailey had gone over this part of what she was going to say at least a dozen times. The words flowed easy as the Mississippi.

"You are exactly the kind of candidate that we want in our law department here at LSU," he said once she'd finished. "And I can guarantee that the program and the sense of family here at the university will make your time with us years that you will cherish."

Bailey listened and felt like she was on cloud nine. Yes, she had Harvard on a lock, but LSU offered her everything she wanted, as well, and she could stay in Baton Rouge and with Justin.

"It isn't often that we give full-ride scholarships. But with your grades, your statement of purpose essay and of course meeting you…I have no doubt that we made the right decision." He smiled broadly. "And of course any friend of the Lawson family is a friend of ours. One of our biggest benefactors."

Bailey's heart seemed to stop then banged in her chest. "Lawson?"

His face turned almost crimson. He cleared his throat. "Wonderful family," he stuttered.

Bailey felt sick. Justin did this. He arranged for the entire thing. Was her scholarship a real one, or was he paying for that, as well? Her temples began to pound. She pushed up from her seat and extended her hand. "Thank you for your time, Dean Withers."

Before he had the chance to react to his faux pas, Bailey was out the door and practically running down the hallway. How could he do this to her? Manipulate her life? Where would it all end?

Bailey could barely see through the cloud of tears that continued to fill her eyes and the wall of fury that boiled and bubbled up from her stomach. She was giving him back his damned car, his freaking keys and the fairy-tale life that he thought he was going to shove down her throat. She'd called Addison and told her to meet her at Justin's house. Even as Addy pressed, Bailey wouldn't get into details on the phone because she knew that Addy would try to talk her out of it.

Addison had actually beat her there and was parked on the road leading to the entry gate of the house. Bailey slowed and pulled up alongside Addison.

"I'll be right back." She screeched onto Justin's driveway, before Addison could blink, spitting up dirt and dust and came to a halt right at the front step. She snatched her belongings from the passenger seat, got out and stomped up to the front door. She didn't bother to use her key or ring the bell; instead she left the house keys on the mat along with the keys to the Benz. She drew in a shuddering breath, spun away and hurried down the winding walkway and out to the road where Addison was parked.

Bailey tugged the door open and flung herself into the seat. She jammed the seat belt buckle in the slot and folded her arms defiantly in front of her.

Addison knew that when Bailey took that stance and that hot look burned in her eyes, that it was best to keep distant until she was ready to talk. Otherwise one risked getting their head bitten off. She pulled out and got back on the main throughway that led back to their part of town. Periodically, Addison stole furtive glances in Bailey's direction. Her stoic countenance never changed. The suspense was killing her.

"I guess you must know that it's over," Bailey finally said, her voice raw and hoarse.

"I figured as much. But why, B? You were head over heels happy."

"Just proves what I've been saying all along about

relationships—" her voice cracked "—and men wanting to control your life."

"You really sure this is how you want to deal with this?"

"The whole meeting at LSU was manipulated by Justin!" she blurted out, hurtling the conversation in a different direction. "The scholarship, admittance, everything. He used his family name to get me in and pulled the strings to get the full-ride scholarship."

Addison frowned. "And you're pissed…why? Girl, do you have any idea what a lucky damned woman you are?"

"You don't understand, Addy." She folded her arms tighter as images of the trail of uncles drifted across her line of vision, the tears, the breakups, the highs and lows that her mother endured, just to have a man take care of her. No, she would never go down that road, not even for Justin Lawson.

"You're right. I don't understand. The man loves you. You love him. Maybe he shouldn't have pulled strings without telling you, but damn, girl, I know how you are, and I'm sure he does, too. Did it ever occur to you that he did it because he would be crazy lonely without you?"

Bailey pressed her lips together. "Doesn't excuse what he did. And what next? This is my time, my life, my dream, and I'm not going to have anyone twist it to suit themselves. I've held off on doing me for a long time, Addy. This is me time, on my terms, not the me that he wants me to be."

Addison blew out a breath and slowly shook her head. "I still think you're making a big mistake."

"It wouldn't be the first time."

They spent the balance of the drive to Bailey's apartment in silence. Addison pulled up in front of Bailey's building. "Want me to come up?"

"No." She unfastened her seat belt. "I need some time."

"If you want to talk…"

Bailey turned toward her friend and managed a pained

smile. "I know. Thanks for coming." She leaned over and kissed Addison's cheek, then got out of the car.

"Call me!"

Bailey raised her hand in acknowledgment, mounted the three stairs to the front door of her building and went inside. The moment she was safely on the other side of her door and looked around at her life stacked in boxes, the well of tears that she'd held in abeyance, broke loose. She slid down to the floor until she came to rest on her haunches, covered her face with her hands and wept.

Chapter 25

Justin pulled into his driveway and was thrilled but surprised to see the Benz parked right in front of the house. Bailey must have decided to come straight to him after her interview. As he got out of the Lexus, the feelings of happy anticipation began to dissipate. The angle of the car was all wrong, as if it had been thrown to a stop. He walked past the car and up the steps to the front door and saw the house key and the keys to the car tossed on the welcome mat.

Slowly he bent down and picked them up. He turned back to look at the car. Whatever idea he may have had about Bailey being home to greet him was wishful thinking. This was bad, very bad.

Justin put the key in the door and then shut it behind him. The multi-bedroom, two-story mansion echoed with emptiness. The weight of the silence pressed down on him in a way that it had never done before. The enormity of his aloneness bounced off the walls and settled around him.

He pulled off his jacket and tossed it on the chair. He dug his cell phone from his pants pocket and held it in front of him. No matter when he placed the call it wouldn't be good. He pressed number one on the keypad to speed-dial Bailey, and paced the room while he listened to the phone ring until her voice mail came on.

"Bailey, it's me. We need to talk. Call me." He started to hang up. "Please." He disconnected the call then tapped in Carl's number.

"Damn, man. Sounds like you really ticked her off," Carl was saying after hearing what Justin had found when he got home.

"That's an understatement. I had doubts about interfering…"

"But you stopped thinking with your head," Carl said.

"Man, don't go there. It's more than that."

"I know. I know. So what are you going to do?"

"I can't do much of anything until I get to talk to her."

"Maybe you should just go over there. Plead your case, counselor."

"No. If I know Bailey she won't listen. She probably wouldn't let me in." He exhaled.

"Hopefully, she'll call and you two can work it out."

"Yeah," Justin groused, not feeling at all confident.

Justin called Bailey three different times throughout the evening. Each time his call went to voice mail. He could sit in front of her house. She had to come out sometime. Then what? He wouldn't get into a personal squabble on the street. All he could do was wait.

At some point he'd drifted off. Sunrise was making its way above the horizon. He groaned. He'd fallen asleep in the armchair. His muscles were in knots. Then the events of the previous night came flooding back. He snatched up his cell phone that had fallen onto his lap and stared at the face for a list of missed calls. There were no calls, and there were no texts from Bailey. He tossed the phone across the room and ran his hand across his stubbled chin then pushed up from the chair with a mild groan.

Shower and coffee, then he'd figure out what to do next.

"How many times did he call?" Addison asked.

"All together, six."

"B, you need to talk to him."

"There's nothing to talk about, and I'm not going to

give him the opportunity to sweet-talk me into believing that his going behind my back was for my own good."

"Fine. Don't call."

"That's it? You aren't going to badger me to death about calling him?"

"Nope. I'm out of it. This is your decision. You need me to come over and help with anything?"

Bailey sighed. "Everything is done. I called a moving company. They are going to pick up my boxes this afternoon."

"This afternoon!"

"Yes. I decided that I may as well go up there a little earlier and…get settled."

"You really mean get away from Justin and this asshole decision you've made."

"I thought you didn't have anything else to say about it."

"I lied."

"It's part of it," she finally admitted.

"You don't have to do this."

"Yeah, I do. I already called and confirmed the off-campus apartment and paid my deposit over the phone—thanks to the money I got from being fired." The money that Justin had gotten for her. She shook away the thought. "I'm leaving this weekend."

"Bailey! That doesn't give me any time."

"For what?"

"To plan a going-away party or something. You can't just leave like this."

"No fanfare. Just us girls. Promise."

"Okay, my place. Thursday night."

"Sounds fine. I'll be there. I'll call my sisters."

"Love you."

"You, too."

Bailey held the phone to her chest and closed her eyes. She missed him. Deep down to the soles of her feet, she missed him. But she was so angry and disillusioned and betrayed. What he'd done scared her. She knew it was a ridiculous emotion, but she couldn't help it. The idea that Justin had the power to mold the direction of her life, strip her of her independence so that she relied on only him, terrified her.

Getting away was what she had to do. *Justin. Justin. Justin.*

Justin called her at least three times a day for the next four days. He'd sent flowers, cards, text messages. All he wanted to do was talk to her, he'd said. It was most difficult at night when she was alone staring at the crack that ran across her ceiling. She wanted to call him, hear his voice; she wanted to feel his touch, taste him. She wanted to wrap her legs around his broad back and feel him fill her to her throat. Instead, she stared at the crack in the ceiling.

Her apartment was empty of the boxes and clothes that she'd had shipped to her new apartment. Tory got a new job that would pay her a decent salary and pay for her to return to school. Apryl swore that she was going to work on herself before she got involved in another relationship. All things considered, Bailey felt comfortable leaving her siblings. It really seemed like they were going to be able to stand on their own two feet. Of course, she was only a phone call away. It was definitely ladies' night, and Addison was in her element from the spread of food, wine and great music. The girls laughed and shared stories of all of their crazy antics growing up, all the secrets they'd shared, the losses and heartaches.

This was good. This is what she needed, to be reminded that all she'd sacrificed over the years was worth it. Her sisters were going to be fine, and so was she.

The ringing doorbell snapped through the laughter and music.

"The strippers are here!" Tory screeched in delight and gave a high five to Apryl.

Addison left her living room to go to the door. Moments later she returned, and Justin walked in behind her.

Addison, Apryl and Tory all shared a knowing look, offered their greetings and eased out of the room and out to the back deck.

"Hey," Justin said softly. He stuck his hands in his pockets and kept his distance.

Bailey's heart was pounding so loud and so fast, she didn't respond. Justin took a step toward her. "Addison told me that you were leaving tomorrow."

Bailey swallowed and nodded her head.

"You weren't going to say goodbye?"

"Thought I did that already."

The muscles in his face jerked. "I wasn't trying to run your life, Bailey."

"Really? What do you call it when you manipulate and maneuver a situation for your benefit without regard to anyone else?"

"I did it for you, Bailey. And yes, I had selfish reasons." He took a step closer. She curled tighter in her seat. "I didn't want you to leave. I didn't want to risk what we were starting to build. I was wrong." He lowered his head, shaking it slowly. "It was your decision, and I took it away from you." He looked directly into her eyes. "I did it because I love you, and I didn't want to lose you."

Bailey pushed herself up from her seat and walked over to him. "You can't run my life in the name of love, Justin. It will never work between us if you do. I know you have connections and power and money and stuff that I can only imagine, but when we are together it's got to be about us, the decisions made about our relationship have to be made by both of us."

"Whatever you want." He reached out and clasped her shoulders.

His touch thrilled her to the marrow of her bones. Inwardly, she sighed.

"I'm sorry, baby." He stroked her cheek with his finger. "I need you to forgive me. Can you do that? Can you forgive me?" He lifted her chin so that she had to look in his eyes.

"I'll think about it," she taunted.

"It's a start." He slowly lowered his head until his lips touched hers, and the contact shot through him with such force that it pushed his groan of want up from the center of his being and across his lips.

Bailey inhaled his need that fed her own. She sank into his body, and the security of his arms wrapped around her, holding her, assuring her that whatever it would take, he would do.

"I don't know what I would have done if I'd lost you," he murmured against her mouth before tasting the sweetness of the wine on her tongue. "You leave in the morning…" He caressed her waist.

"Yes," she managed as he trailed kisses along her neck.

"Then we don't have much time. Come home with me."

"What about…" She jerked her head toward the back deck.

"Believe me, they'll understand. Get your things."

It was clear that it wasn't a question. It was a statement. But this time she didn't care that he wasn't asking what she wanted, but telling her what she needed—a night with the man that she loved.

Chapter 26

"If it's okay with you, I'll fly you up in the morning."

Bailey sighed and stretched her limbs that had gotten a serious workout from the moment they'd crossed the threshold of his home. She smiled in the darkness. "I'd like that."

"So glad that you approve, Ms. Sinclair." He chuckled and caressed her bare hip, and the simple action had him growing hard again. "Hmm. Turn on your stomach," he said deep in her ear.

Bailey glanced at him then turned onto her stomach.

Justin pulled one of the overstuffed down pillows from the top of the bed and pushed it under Bailey's pelvis, raising her round derriere to bring it closer. He kissed the back of her neck, nibbled her ears and stroked the curve of her spine with his tongue until she was one electrified nerve. He reached between her and the pillow and toyed with the hard bud of her sex until her body shuddered, and her soft whimpers rose to cries, begging him to make her come.

"Not yet," he whispered. His fingers played with her until they were slick with her need, and then he entered her in one deep thrust that forced the air out of her lungs. He grabbed her hips to control exactly how fast and how deep he wanted things to go. She was totally at his mercy. He took his time to make her beg for release. And she did, again and again.

* * *

"I've never been on a private plane," Bailey said as she stepped on board. She had to admit, even if not to Justin, that this beat flying commercial any day.

"Make yourself comfortable." He stowed their carry-on luggage in the overhead bins.

A flight attendant came by with a tray of refreshments. Bailey opted for an iced tea and settled down into the plush leather seat. "Do you know how to fly?"

"Mmm-hmm." He buckled his belt, turned to her and grinned.

"What else do I need to know about you?"

Justin grinned. "We have years to unwrap all of my secrets."

"I like the sound of that…years."

"So do I."

When they landed in Boston, Justin had a car waiting for them to take them to her new apartment. They stopped at the management office where she picked up her keys.

The apartment was just like the pictures, open and airy with modern touches. The one bedroom was small but cozy, and there was a small terrace that added a bit of ambiance. The delivery company had brought in all of the boxes. Her new bed was being delivered, so for the time being she'd have to sleep on the pullout couch that came with the apartment.

"This is nice," Justin said, looking around and taking inventory. "I'm going to like staying here."

"Staying here?"

"I thought I'd wait until you got here before I told you."

"Told me what, Justin?"

"I'm going to be relocating…to Boston. My work, The

Justice Project, can succeed from here as well as from Baton Rouge. Carl can handle things on that end."

"Justin..."

"I know you have this thing about anyone other than you moving the puzzle pieces of your life around. But this time, Bailey—" he stepped up to her "—I'm making an executive decision for the both of us. Now, if you have a problem with that, tell me now."

Her heart thundered, and her soul swelled with happiness. She stepped into his arms. "Whatever you say, Mr. Lawson."

He pulled her tight and sealed their pact with a kiss.

* * * * *

Two classic novels featuring the sexy and sensational Westmoreland family…

SPARKS OF TEMPTATION

New York Times **Bestselling Author** **BRENDA JACKSON**

The moment Jason Westmoreland meets Bella Bostwick in *The Proposal*, he wants her—and the land she's inherited. With one convenient proposal, he could have the Southern beauty in his bed and her birthright in his hands. But that's only if Bella says yes…

The affair between Dr. Micah Westmoreland and Kalina Daniels ended too abruptly. Now that they are working side by side, he can't ignore the heat that still burns between them. And he plans to make her his… in *Feeling the Heat*.

"Jackson's love scenes are hot and steamy and her storyline believable enough to make readers beg for more."
—*RT Book Reviews* on *PRIVATE ARRANGEMENTS*

Available February 2015 wherever books are sold!

www.Harlequin.com

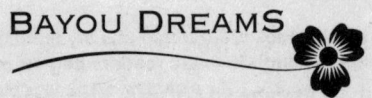

REQUEST YOUR FREE BOOKS!

2 FREE NOVELS PLUS 2 FREE GIFTS!

KIMANI ROMANCE ™

Love's ultimate destination!

A road trip to love…

JOURNEY *To* SEDUCTION

CANDACE SHAW

Sydney Chase has been driving attorney Bryce Monroe crazy. No one else combines tough and tender in such a sexy, irresistible package. Though Syd has him pegged as a spoiled brat, a spur-of-the-moment Vegas road trip is Bryce's one chance to prove otherwise. Yet what happens in Vegas is impossible to forget, and Bryce isn't letting go until he's crashed through every single one of her defenses…

★★★ CHASING LOVE

www.Harlequin.com

Available February 2015 wherever books are sold!

KPCS3920215